DON WINSLOW OF THE NAVY

"JUST HOLD THAT POSE, SAILOR!" BARKED THE STOCKY
LIEUTENANT.

DON WINSLOW
OF THE NAVY

by

FRANK V. MARTINEK

Illustrated by

F. WARREN

WILDSIDE PRESS

CONTENTS

CHAPTER		PAGE

DON WINSLOW OF THE NAVY

DON WINSLOW OF THE NAVY

I

BOMBED!

On the white sand of a jungle bordered cove, two men and a girl stood gazing seaward, their eyes shielded against the rising sun's first beams. To judge by their torn, mudstained clothing, they had been meeting hardship in large, tough chunks. Out here on the beach they would soon face more of it, when the sun grew hot enough to broil a white man's skin.

The slim, dark-eyed girl had suffered less, apparently, than her two companions. Yet her stout whipcord breeches showed rough wear, and her face, under a mass of wind blown curls, bore traces of weariness and jungle dirt. The society columnist who had described her coiffure at a Washington ball, six weeks ago, would have been startled to recognize Mercedes Colby, daugher of a retired Navy Admiral.

Even more sharply would that columnist have been astonished by the identity of Miss Colby's present escorts. For United States Naval Commanders are not ordinarily found in beachcombers' rags, on the shore of a tropical island. And nothing in the book of Navy

Regulations (which covers everything) decrees that even a lieutenant must tackle the Haitian jungle barefooted, with half a shirt tucked into the remnant of once-white trousers.

The truth was that ordinary duties had never been the lot of Don Winslow and his husky shadow Lieutenant "Red" Pennington since their appointment to the Naval Intelligence Service. In a few adventure-packed months they had learned to take hardships as a daily ration, with danger for spice. Hunger, exhaustion, blistered skin and bleeding feet, were small matters compared with the importance of their present job —the stamping out of a vast international crime ring, whose deliberate aim was to plunge the whole world into war.

To combat this secret menace the United States Government had needed an officer of rare courage and ability for its chief field operative, a man able to match wits with the world's greatest spymaster—and win! He must be highly skilled in all forms of combat, an expert with every type of weapon. He must be tireless, self-reliant, and prepared to give his life in the line of duty, without warning and without regret. With these qualities in mind, the Navy Department's final choice had fallen upon an already distinguished young officer —Commander Don Winslow.

Not all of history's great adventurers have looked their parts; but Don Winslow in the ragged ruin of his uniform whites was still a man to draw attention. The lithe swing of his powerfully muscled body, from shoulders to lean hips—the unconscious air of command which marks a Navy officer—the clear, level gaze and the strong line of his jaw—all stamped him as a superb product of American birth and training.

Red Pennington, Don's inseparable companion, cut a far less heroic figure. Except for gorilla-like strength evident beneath his fat, the young lieutenant would have resembled a chubby clown. Just now his naturally tender skin was tortured by sunburn and insect bites to the consistency of raw beef; yet its lumpy redness gave an irresistible effect of comic makeup. Fortunately Red's own sense of humor was unconquerable and almost as deep as his loyalty to Don Winslow. These two traits, plus real ability as an officer and fighting man, had won him the coveted job of Don's most trusted assistant, and the envy of every young naval officer who preferred adventure to routine.

Time and again, both Don Winslow and Red had been marked for death by the secret organization of Scorpia, whose warmaking plots they had more than once uncovered and wrecked. Their great hope was to capture or destroy the crime ring's despotic master— that evil, elusive genius who called himself merely "The Scorpion" and sucked in through a thousand agents the war-poisoned wealth of nations. Wherever war, or the fear of it, created topheavy armaments the Scorpion's brood took their fat share of graft and hush money. War and murder were Scorpia's stock in trade, and to enlarge them its members' perverted souls were pledged.

So great had the Scorpion's secret power become when the United States Government first realized its danger, that only by a miracle could the threat of war be lifted from our own and neighbor nations. In this crisis Don Winslow was chosen to go out, like David against the giant Goliath, and end the Scorpion's menace.

Flying over the Windward Passage, Don and Red finally spotted and bombed the Scorpion's submarine which had been torpedoing United States war vessels. A short time later mysterious anti-aircraft fire brought their plane down in the coastal jungle of Haiti. Neither officer was hurt, however, and the gunners from the Scorpion submarine base found the tables suddenly turned when Don and Red surprised them and siezed their hidden stronghold. In the fight one Scorpion agent was killed. The others escaped, under cover of darkness.

Amazement struck the two young officers when they discovered their close friend and childhood playmate, Mercedes Colby, a prisoner in the enemy's underground quarters. Mercedes had blundered upon the Scorpion base, after being shipwrecked on the wild Haitian coast. With her had been taken prisoner a Spanish-American, Yanos, two native fishermen, and an ex-Navy seaman by the name of Jerry Ward.

At the present moment all but Mercedes, Don and Red were asleep in the immense underground tank which the enemy had used as supply base and living quarters. Knowing that the Commander had radioed for a gunboat to pick them up, they took it for granted that their troubles were over.

However, the three young persons now looking out to sea knew better than to take anything for granted where the evil power of Scorpia was involved. By this time the failure of his men to report would have warned the Scorpion that his submarine base was captured. His counterattack might be delayed, but it was certain to be deadly.

With real relief therefore the two officers and Mercedes recognized the trim lines of the United States Gunboat *Gatoon,* just rounding a nearby headland. As the converted yacht's bower anchor splashed down at the cove's mouth, her launch swung outboard from the davits, manned by a boatswain and two armed sailors. At the same time a two-seater flying boat roared in out of the dawn to land like a white gull in the offing.

"That was quick answer to your radio call, Don!" observed Red Pennington as the *Gatoon's* launch drove swiftly shoreward. "I didn't count on their raising this little jungle cove till noon. But, say! I sure hope Cap'n Riggs has got more than Java and sinkers for breakfast!"

Don Winslow nodded, watching the launch's bow touch lightly on the white beach. It seemed that for a little while the three of them could exchange dangers and hardships for a well-earned rest aboard ship. The Navy boatswain who had just leaped ashore was a welcome symbol of America's armed yet peace-loving might, ready at all times to protect its loyal citizens.

Answering the warrant officer's salute, Don indicated the anchored seaplane.

"Whose craft is that?" he queried. "It's not a Navy boat!"

"It's Mr. Splendor's private plane, sir," answered the boatswain. "A young fellow called Panama is piloting him. They spotted you at first crack of dawn and led us in to this cove."

"That sounds like Michael Splendor!" exclaimed Mercedes Colby. "He's always one jump ahead of everyone else in the Naval Intelligence. Except Don, of course. The man is a wonder...."

She broke off in alarm, as the drone of an approaching airplane grew on the morning air.

"There's another plane!" she cried, clutching at Commander Winslow's arm. "Don, do you think it could be a Scorpion scout, coming back to investigate?"

"It could be!" the young officer decided swiftly. "In any case, this changes our plans. Boatswain! Shove off at once in the launch with Miss Colby. Get her safely aboard the gunboat and then come back. Lieutenant Pennington and I will evacuate the other men from the underground base. Hurry, Red!"

He turned and raced up the beach, followed by the stocky junior officer. Two minutes later he paused at the rim of a huge steel cylinder whose bulk appeared to be sunk deep in the earth. Thick jungle growth had sprawled across the great tank's top, hiding it completely from the beach.

One hand on the hatchway leading to the cylinder's

interior, Don Winslow waited for his friend to catch up.

"What in thunder's all the hurry, Don?" the red-headed lieutenant gasped, stumbling through the underbrush. "Even if that is a Scorpion plane up there, it wouldn't dare attack the gunboat!"

"Maybe not," replied Don Winslow, jerking open the hatch. "But I wouldn't be surprised if they tried dropping a bomb on this secret base, now that we've captured it. There's a lot of priceless equipment here— new gadgets of the Scorpion's own invention. He'd rather destroy that stuff than let us take it away. That's why I want to get every man out of here before it's too late!"

A narrow steel ladder led down into the cylinder. In the darkness, its slender rungs offered tricky footing, but the two Navy men made short work of the descent. Thirty feet below the hatchway, they reached a dimly lighted landing, from which two doors opened.

"Take the berth deck, Red," Don directed curtly. "Get Yanos and the two native fishermen out of their hammocks and up the ladder. I'll bring Jerry from the chartroom. If he's still unconscious I'll carry him topside."

"Aye-aye, Skipper!" muttered Red Pennington, pushing through the left-hand door. "If you need any help, just sing out!"

A short corridor led Don Winslow to the cylinder's crowded chartroom, where the seaman, Jerry Ward, lay on a cot between two banks of electrical apparatus.

Don glanced with envious eyes at the array of super-sensitive instruments.

"If only we had time to get some of this stuff aboard the gunboat!" he muttered. "No time to think about that now, though. That plane overhead may lay an 'egg' on this place any minute!"

Bending over the unconscious Jerry, he shook the man gently. There was no response. A head wound, received at the time of his capture, had left the plucky fellow hanging between life and death.

Carefully Don lifted the limp body in his arms and turned to the door. As he did so, a muffled explosion shook the steel walls about him.

Bursting out onto the lower landing, Don Winslow collided with Lieutenant Pennington.

"Quick, Red!" he barked. "Take Jerry on your back, and get up that ladder. I'll lash his wrists together, so you'll have both hands free to climb with. Where are Yanos and the others?"

"They've just gone up!" Red answered, stooping to take Jerry's weight. "And say! That *did* sound like a bomb overhead, just now! We'd better get out of here in a hurry!"

"Right!" grunted Don, pushing the other toward the ladder. "You take Jerry up and get him down to the boat. I've got a little job to do before I follow you; so don't wait."

"But, Don!" protested the red-haired officer. "I can't leave you here. . . ."

"On your way, Lieutenant!" snapped the young commander. "Obey orders and get that seaman down to the boat. Lively, now!"

Talking to himself in a bitter undertone, Red Pennington toiled up the ladder with his heavy burden. He'd obey those orders, all right, but Don hadn't forbidden him to return after seeing Jerry safely in the boat. If his commanding officer was going to stick around where the bombs were dropping, a certain husky lieutenant meant to share the danger with him!

Meantime, Don Winslow had returned to the chartroom, and was hastily disconnecting the main electric cables leading to the Scorpion's weather mapping machine.

The invention was priceless, if it could be salvaged. Heavy as it was, Don thought he might be able to carry it up the ladder.

As he worked, with flashlight and screwdriver, wrench and pliers, two more bomb explosions shook the underground base.

Little by little, a stifling, smoky odor filled the air of the chartroom. Tears filled Don's smarting eyes, inflamed by the acrid fumes. His breath came raspingly between dry coughs.

Reluctantly he dropped his tools and fumbled for the doorknob.

"Those were *gas* bombs, not TNT!" he mumbled thickly, as he stumbled from the room. "Smoke's coming down the hatch. Got to get up where there's some —uh—air to breathe!"

As he groped toward the ladder a bulky form emerged from the smoke above him.

"Don! Don, old man!" came Red Pennington's choking cry.

"Right here, Red!" coughed Don Winslow, clinging to the ladder's lower rungs. "I'm—uh—all right. Coming up now. But you shouldn't have come back!"

"Thank heaven, you're okay!" the redhead replied. "Want me to give you a hand?"

"No! I'll make it. Hustle, now, or the smoke is going to—uh—get us both! Where're Mercedes and Jerry?"

Pennington's answer was a coughing fit, which shook the steel ladder. Just below him, Don Winslow gripped the narrow rungs and gasped for breath. After a moment the two men resumed their painful climb, fighting against a growing dizziness.

"Mercedes—Jerry—on the beach!" came Red's muffled words. "Smoke too thick to see—see the boat. Got to save breath now, and—uh—climb!"

II

OUT OF THE POISON FOG

Over the jungle cove rolled an unbroken cloud of billowing, greenish smoke. It blotted out the white beach, spread out over the blue water, and crept slowly outward toward the anchored gunboat.

From its murky edge came the roar of powerful engines. The seaplane's nose emerged from the poisonous smoke, slid swiftly over the waves, and rose like a great white gull into the clear upper air.

Aboard the gunboat, steam winches began weighing the two anchors, while officers and seamen hurried to batten down hatches and close ventilators. Slowly the craft's sharp bow swung seaward. Her twin propellors churned white water at her stern.

Neither the launch nor its erstwhile occupants could be seen beneath that greenish cloud of poison gas. In vain the seaplane's pilot circled the big airship over the jungle's edge, looking for a break in the smoke.

"Fly lower, Panama!" commanded the hard-jawed man in the after cockpit. "If that stuff thins, even for a moment, we may be able to spot somebody. There's eleven souls down there, at death's door for all we know."

"That's where we'll be, Mr. Splendor, if the gas hits

us!" replied the pilot. "But here goes. . . . Look! The wind's made a rift in the cloud! There's the launch, and a couple of men sprawled beside it!"

"Drop landing gear!" cried Splendor, as the plane's nose dipped earthward. "Land in the cove and taxi right up onto the beach. We must get those poor fellows to the gunboat or die trying!"

With a quick nod, Panama cut the throttle. An instant later the seaplane's pontoons touched the water in a flash of white spray. Straight into the thinning gas cloud the ship plunged, heading for the level beach.

To anxious watchers aboard the gunboat, it looked as if Michael Splendor and his plucky pilot had committed deliberate suicide. Unable to see the rift which Panama had spotted from the air, they waited in agonized suspense for the plane's reappearance.

Suddenly Captain Riggs raised a pointing arm.

"There's the plane, now, but something's wrong, Lieutenant!" he exclaimed, to the junior officer beside him. "See how low she rides in the water! And what under the sun are those dark blotches on the forward fuselage?"

Peering through his binoculars, Lieutenant Darnley cried out in amazement.

"They're men, Captain!" he reported. "Mr. Splendor is holding two of them, and there's another in his cockpit. All three look to be unconscious, sir!"

"Lower the whaleboat!" bellowed Riggs, leaning over the bridge's rail. "Stand by to take men off the seaplane. Darnley, tell the medical officer to prepare berths in the sick bay. I'm going in the boat myself!"

Moments later the seaplane's crew gave up their helpless passengers to the whaleboat. Michael Splendor, his eyes streaming with tears from the poison gas fumes, insisted on going back at once for another rescue attempt.

"We've still to find the main shore party, Captain!" he explained between gasps for breath. "There's young Winslow and Pennington still to be found, not to forget Admiral Colby's daughter. Every second will count if we're to save their lives!"

"You're right, Mr. Splendor!" agreed Riggs, balancing in the whaleboat's sternsheets. "We'll follow you inshore, as soon as we get these poor fellows aboard. The smoke looks to be thinning now. Good luck!"

His words were drowned out by the roar of the seaplane's motors. Like a huge water bird she taxied around, heading back to the beach. At the same moment, the boat's oarsmen gave way with short powerful strokes that sped them toward the waiting ship.

Once alongside, the boat falls were made fast by expert hands, and the whaleboat was lifted dripping from the water. Even before the gassed seamen were transferred to the sick bay, the ship was nosing shoreward to join in the next desperate attempt at rescuing Don Winslow and his gallant companions.

Many hours later a westering sun cast its mellow rays through the portholes of the gunboat *Gatoon,* now a floating hospital anchored off the coast of Haiti. In the vessel's sick bay, a white-coated medical officer bent frowning over one of the ten occupied berths. So intently was he watching the patient that he failed to hear the door open, or see the approach of the big man in the wheel chair.

"I thought this is where I'd find you, Doctor!" exclaimed the latter, his tone warm with a touch of Irish brogue. "They told me the seaman, Jerry, is sinking fast!"

The young doctor turned with a shake of his head.

"He's in pretty bad shape, Mr. Splendor," he said wearily. "The others are coming around surprisingly well, though. Even the girl, Miss Colby. I expect Commander Winslow and Lieutenant Pennington will regain consciousness this evening."

"That's just fine, Doctor!" exclaimed Splendor heartily. "Do ye mind if I go along when next ye look in on 'em. Even with me crippled legs, I promise not to be in the way."

"Come along, of course, Mr. Splendor," smiled the medical officer, opening the door. "If you and your seaplane had been OUT of the way this morning, none of these men would be alive now. You're pretty much of a hero on this ship, whether you know it or not!"

"You mean my pilot, Panama!" growled the big man, rolling his chair along the steel deck. "It was him who did the rescuing, while I sat helpless in me cockpit. . . . Ah! So this is the cabin where ye put Don Winslow and his redheaded mate, eh?"

With a nod, the doctor threw open the cabin door.

"They seem to be still asleep, both of them," he murmured, glancing across the narrow room. "Here! I'll help you with that chair, if you'd like to come in."

Low pitched as they were, the words registered on Don Winslow's slumbering senses. He stirred, opened his eyes, and struggled up on one elbow.

"Michael Splendor!" he exclaimed huskily. "I dreamed about you, and a seaplane, and a cloud of poison smoke and . . . Say! Where are we, anyhow? And what am I doing in this cabin?"

Rolling his chair swiftly to the side of the berth, Michael Splendor held up a big hand.

"Whisht, and be quiet, young feller-me-lad!" he rumbled. "It was no dream ye had about the poison smoke. Ye're still sick from it, so take it easy. Your mate, the redheaded lieutenant, is sleepin' in the next berth to ye."

"I am not, Don!" croaked Red Pennington, trying to sit up. "I was lying low so as not to wake you! Oh-h-h! Golly! Does my head hurt!"

"It will be worse if you don't lie down, Pennington!" snapped the medical officer. "If you and Commander Winslow didn't have leather lungs and cast iron constitutions, we'd be sewing you up in canvas right now, for a sea burial. You two got the biggest dose of smoke!"

"But Mercedes—I mean, Miss Colby—she must have been gassed too!" cried Don Winslow, from the other berth. "Is she coming out of it yet, Doctor? Tell me the truth. . . ."

"Hush, lad!" soothed Splendor, pushing the young officer back onto his pillow. "Miss Colby's out of danger, so don't excite yourself. We got Yanos and the two fishermen in time, too, along with the launch's crew. Ye'll hear all the details tomorrow, when you're feelin' stronger. The doctor and I will be leavin' ye now."

"But—the underground base!" muttered Don weakly, pressing a hand to his aching eyes. "About that apparatus, and the automatic weather map— Tell me, Splendor. . . ."

"We'll talk about that another time," said the man in the wheel chair. "There's nothing to worry about, except the strength ye're wastin' this minute, Commander. So pipe down and give your thoughts a rest till ye're called on deck. The same goes for you, Pennington, d'ye hear?"

"Aye-aye, sir!" came the redhead's mumbled response, as the cabin door closed softly behind the visitors.

III

HIGH EXPLOSIVE

Dawn had just broken the following day when Don Winslow sat up on the edge of his berth. There was a light of determination in his eye, and a fighting set to his unshaven jaw.

He was going to get up, shave and dress before the ship's doctor had a chance to forbid him. He was tired of lying in a berth. Most of all, he was anxious to see for himself if Mercedes and the others were really getting over the effects of the poison gas.

There were some difficulties to be met, of course. In the first place, his head was still woozy, and the deck heaved up and down as if in heavy weather. In the second place, someone had taken away his torn and muddy uniform. If he could get to the locker in the corner, though, he might find something to put on.

Groping his way along the bulkhead, Don reached the locker and jerked open the door. There, as he had hoped, hung an officer's spare uniform, along with a dress sword, weapon belt and other equipment. A drawer beneath contained underwear, shaving kit, and towels.

The set-up was complete, including a hot water tap

in another corner of the cabin. If only Red didn't wake up, or the doctor come in before he was dressed. . . .

Fifteen minutes later Don was buttoning up his borrowed tunic, when a sudden yell and a thump spun him around in alarm.

"Sufferin' sea serpents!" gurgled the voice of Red Pennington.

More muffled groans, grunts and howls for help issued from the tangle of bedclothes under Red's berth. Don came to the rescue, laughing so hard that he almost lost his footing.

"Boy! You sure hit the deck in a hurry!" he chuckled, unwinding a sheet from around his stocky friend's neck. "What were you dreaming about, anyway, to make you yell like that?"

"A-argh! Umph!" groaned Red, feeling of his chafed neck. "It's no laughing matter, if you want to know it! I dreamed the Scorpion's men were hanging me to the yardarm, and you came along just in time to cut me down. What if it *was* only a sheet instead of a rope? That dream was real enough!"

"It probably was," agreed Don Winslow, his grin fading. "I had nightmares aplenty myself. It must be the effects of that poison wearing off. You'll feel better if you get up and shave, Red. Unfortunately, I have on the only uniform in the cabin. . . ."

"Unfortunately is right,—if you refer to the fit!" cut in the fat lieutenant sourly as he got to his feet. "That tunic you've got on was built for a man of ample girth. Like me, for instance! And as for the pants—Whee-ew! Don't let the wind catch 'em un-furled, when you go topside, Commander! That's all I say!"

"And it'll be enough, too, Lieutenant. At least until I get my own clothes back!" retorted Don, moving over to the open porthole. "Anyhow, this suit covers me better than— Whoa, there! Careful, sailor! Those knees of yours are going to buckle right under you!"

Catching Red's arm, Don Winslow steadied him just in time.

"Where were you going to walk to, shipmate?" he asked.

Pennington's reply was shaky, despite his plucky grin.

"Across to that chair and then collapse!" he answered. "Boy, oh, boy—this room's going around! I'm weak as a baby. Hope it'll pass off before Doc orders me back to bed."

"Hope so, Red!" replied Don, easing his friend into the chair. "We'll just sit here and talk for a few minutes. You know, I wish Headquarters hadn't ordered us to destroy the Scorpion's base, here. I hate to blow up all the machinery there that's too heavy to move. If only I had another month to study those new inventions!"

"Okay, Commander!" chuckled Red Pennington. "Why don't you dig up the whole underground base and take it along as a souvenir? That'd be just as reasonable as— Say, listen, Skipper! You ought to be more than satisfied with what you've done already.

Wasn't it you that found the Scorpion's base, to begin with? And who else but Don Winslow discovered how our ships were destroyed, here in the Windward Passage? It was you, more than anybody else, who pulled the last trick of sinking the Scorpion's submarine. What more do you want, to be happy?"

Don Winslow turned to gaze out of the porthole at the sunlit waves of the cove. Beyond stretched the white sand beach, now swarming with sailors in dungarees.

The *Gatoon's* launch and two whaleboats were pulled up at the edge of the water. Don guessed that they were getting ready to blow up the great steel cylinder buried at the jungle's edge. In a few hours, at most, the gunboat would be weighing anchor, bound for the safety of civilized ports.

Which was all as it should be; and yet. . . .

"If the truth has to be told, Red," the young commander said softly, "I'll never be satisfied until I nab the biggest prize of all—the Scorpion himself. Anything less than wiping out that menace to world peace, falls short of victory. You know how deeply I feel about that!"

"I do; and you're not alone in that feeling!" responded Pennington earnestly. "But remember, Skipper, the capture of the Scorpion is nearer today than it was six months ago. Through *your* efforts his secret organization is now on the defensive—almost on the run. I may not be a prophet or anything like that, but

I'll bet my life that within six months' time you'll have the Scorpion across the table from you—a prisoner!"

For a long moment Don Winslow gazed straight into his friend's eager face. Red's praise, his confidence, his enthusiasm, were all exaggerated, perhaps. All the same they meant a lot just at this time. The young commander's chest expanded with a sigh of unspoken gratitude to this loyal friend and shipmate.

"You're sure a grand tonic, Red, old man!" he smiled. "I hope your prediction comes true, to the letter. But we've got to do something more than just hope and wish, you know!"

"I do know, Don!" replied the chubby officer soberly. "And I've been doing a lot of thinking in the last few hours. There's an idea that came to me last night. Maybe you'll say it's all crazy, but. . . ."

"Crazy ideas are sometimes the best, after all, Red," Don encouraged, as Pennington hesitated. "Let's have it, anyhow. We can't afford to overlook any bets in this man's game, so shoot!"

Red Pennington wriggled uneasily in his chair.

"Well—all right. You asked for it, so don't laugh!" he blurted finally. "It's just this: you know enough right now to pass yourself off as one of the Scorpion's agents. You actually did it, for a short while, the time we barged in on Shilling and the Shark,—remember? Why couldn't you do it again, and make it stick?"

Don Winslow took a turn up and down the cabin's narrow space, frowning as he chewed mentally on

Red's suggestion. Bringing up before his friend's chair, he shook his head smilingly.

"It wouldn't do, shipmate," he stated. "In the first place, we'd have to capture some member of Scorpia who looked enough like me to make my disguise and substitution possible. Next, I'd have to find a way to open that man's mind out flat, and memorize everything he knew. It's all very well to dream about, but you know yourself such breaks only come once in a lifetime."

"Unless you make 'em, Skipper!" returned the stocky lieutenant, pushing himself up to his feet. "For instance, you could get yourself kicked out of the Navy —dishonorably discharged—stripped of your commission—disgraced publicly before your shipmates. Suppose you did that, and were determined to get revenge on the Navy for breaking you. Just where, then, would you be most likely to turn for help? Answer me, Don!"

For ten seconds the young commander stood gaping in stark amazement at the wildness of Red Pennington's scheme. Slowly his expression changed to a boyish grin.

"I get you now, Red!" he said admiringly. "For sheer, crazy daring, your idea takes the cake. It's fantastic, goofy, impossible, and yet—the more I think about it the more it grows on me, sailor! We'll talk it over with Michael Splendor in any case, and see. . . ."

With a sudden leap, Don Winslow cleared the space to the cabin door and yanked it violently open. A crouched figure outside dodged back, ducking around a corner. The officer sprang after him, only to trip and go sprawling in the "cabin country" just outside.

Ruefully he got to his feet and re-entered the door, closing it after him.

"Looks as if that poison gas left my legs kind of wobbly, too!" he grumbled, seating himself on his berth. "I almost caught Mr. Snooper at that. But, Red! You see what this means? *There's at least one Scorpion spy aboard this vessel!* He probably got an earful of our conversation, too, and. . . ."

"BOO-OOM! BR-ROM-BOOM!"

The heavy explosions came from somewhere inshore. Red Pennington leaped from his chair to join Don Winslow at the cabin's porthole. They were in time to see a huge mushroom of earth and water rise high over the jungle at the edge of the little cove.

Closer to the ship, and traveling nearer at appalling speed, rose a low wall of water—a miniature tidal wave created by the blast. As it struck the *Gatoon's* port bow, the decks tilted crazily, like those of a toy boat. After the wave had passed there came a dull roar of water rushing into a vast crater in the cove's white beach.

"The underground base!" breathed Red, clinging weakly to the porthole. "They've blown it up, Don, along with all that machinery the Scorpion's agents left behind!"

IV

THE CODE MESSAGE

Stepping back, Don Winslow stared at his friend aghast.

"Not everything—not ALL the machinery, I hope, Red!" he groaned. "Man alive! The Scorpion's weather mapping machine alone was a priceless invention. If they've blown that up—"

"They didn't, Commander, so put your mind at rest!" interrupted the rich brogue of Michael Splendor from the doorway. "I hope you'll forgive me for wheelin' in on ye unexpected, gentlemen. What with the explosions and the pitchin' of the ship in that tidal wave, 'tis no wonder ye didn't hear me knock!"

Don Winslow turned to grip the crippled man's big hand.

"We'll forgive you, Mr. Splendor," he smiled, "provided you tell us what's been happening ashore since yesterday. By the looks of the gang on the beach, a little while ago, there was a lot of work going on—more than just laying a dynamite charge."

"There was indeed!" nodded Splendor. "Captain Riggs' lads have been workin' the whole night tryin' to salvage the machines of the Scorpion's invention. They've got most of them aboard ship now, includin"

24

your precious weather map. What they blew up just now was little more than an empty shell. I came in especially to tell ye that, and to bring ye this bundle before the doctor comes in to bother ye."

With a broad wink, the big man produced a large package from under the blanket which covered his crippled legs. Ripping off the paper wrapping, he disclosed a pair of officer's uniforms.

"I had to guess at the sizes when I borrowed them, lads," he chuckled, "but they should fit better than what ye're wearin' at present. Look under the after part of me wheel chair for another bundle of shirts, shoes, and whatnot. Ye see, I thought if the doctor saw ye both dressed and about the decks he'd not have the heart to order ye back to bed. I know how hard it is for an active man to be kept on his back when there's work to do!"

Don Winslow took the package of clothing in wordless gratitude. Somehow, this middle aged cripple's thoughtfulness touched him more deeply than he could express.

Lieutenant Pennington's pleasure, however, was quite outspoken.

"You're a lifesaver, Mr. Splendor!" he cried, seizing the bundle out of Don's hands. "I'd have died of shame if I'd had to finish this voyage in a bathrobe and pajamas. I feel a hundred per cent better already. Just wait till I get these on. . . ."

"What news of Miss Colby, and the seaman Jerry?" asked Don, as Red retreated behind the locker door.

"That is, if it's not too early for the doctor's report."

"They're both on the mend," replied Splendor, his blue eyes twinkling. "Especially the young lady. Her cabin door was open as I came by, and I heard her askin' the medical officer when you would be well enough to take her for a stroll on deck! But that isn't all the news I have to tell ye, Commander. Lieutenant Darnley brought back a bundle of papers from the chartroom of the underground base. Unless my old eyes deceive me, there's one item among them the Scorpion would prefer we didn't know about."

Don, seated on the edge of his berth, leaned forward tensely, his eyes alight.

"Great work, Mr. Splendor!" he exclaimed. "Red Pennington and I went through those papers in a hurry without finding a thing of interest. What was it you picked out?"

"A mere bit of paper tucked away in a small notebook," answered the cripple, fumbling in a pocket of his loose coat. " 'Tis no wonder ye overlooked it; but with me nose for smellin' out secret codes, I was suspicious of the thing immediately. Now, then—here it is! An innocent-looking message, is it not? But with the code key right there in the notebook, it becomes something else entirely."

Red Pennington, now dressed in a fresh shirt and trousers which fitted him surprisingly well, edged up to the wheel chair. His eyes were fairly popping with curiosity and excitement.

"G-golly!" he said huskily. "To think we both had

this note in our hands, and never suspected anything queer! Mind if I look over your shoulder, Don?"

"Read it aloud, Lieutenant!" urged Michael Splendor, glancing up with a nod.

Red Pennington bent closer.

" 'Proceed with original contract,' " he read, " 'for delivery October or not later than the first of the year. We will expect San Francisco order on schedule as this Empire contact is highly important. Our telegraph operator advises that many messages suggest Cho-San as the ideal sales name for our delightful produce which suggests China Seas and that catchy name brings orders.' "

"Say, Don!" the red-haired lieutenant commented. "If that's in code, it's a loo-loo! Sounds just like an ordinary business letter, or something!"

"You're right, so it does!" chuckled Michael Splendor. "But there's the catch. Ye note that the message is typed in five word lines. Very well, take this pencil and cross out all but the first word in the first line, the second word in the second line, and so on through the fifth. At the sixth line begin again with the first word. When ye've finished, read me what ye have left."

With a low whistle of comprehension, Don Winslow took the pencil and, stepping over to the cabin's desk, swiftly made the indicated changes. A few seconds later, he read off slowly the words which remained:

" 'Proceed—October—first—San Francisco—Empire

—contact—Operator—Cho-San—for—China Seas—orders.' "

"Well, I'll be keelhauled!" blurted Red Pennington. "That's a Scorpion message, all right. It sounds plain enough, too, except for the word 'Empire' and 'Cho-San.' Do they make any sense to you, Mr. Splendor?"

The man in the wheel chair did not reply. While Don had been decoding the message, the cripple had moved his rubber tired vehicle over to the porthole. He was now gazing out at the sunlit shore line, with an expression of grim thoughtfulness.

Following the man's look, Don gave a start of amazement.

"Why, the shore seems to be moving!" he exclaimed. "I didn't realize the ship was under way, did you, Red? We were both so interested in this code message. Where are we bound, Mr. Splendor?"

With a quick movement, the big man whirled his chair about, and faced the two young officers. His broad, lined face had the look of a person just waking from a heavy sleep.

"Excuse me, gentlemen!" he said apologetically. "I'm afraid me mind was far away when ye spoke. The name 'Cho-San' recalled things I'd like to forget, if this broken body of mine would let me. But this is no time to talk of me own troubles! Ye asked where we were bound, did ye not?"

At Don's silent nod, Michael Splendor's mood underwent another swift change. His strikingly blue eyes lighted with their irresistible smile.

"We're steerin' for Port-au-Prince," he stated. " 'Tis meself persuaded Captain Riggs to put us ashore there for a few days, while we're waitin' fresh orders from Washington. I've a big, cool, country residence of me own near the city, where ye and Miss Colby will be more than welcome to stay and recover ye're full health. Don't refuse, now, and disappoint an old shut-in who has little to live for except his friends!"

"Don't worry!" laughed Don Winslow, exchanging glances with Red. "We've heard plenty about your famous country house, Mr. Splendor, and we're not refusing! It's more like a palace than an ordinary dwelling, I understand."

"That's fine, Commander," said Splendor, wheeling himself around toward the door. "And now, if ye'll just hand me that code letter from the desk, I'll be shovin' off."

Red Pennington stepped over to the desk, only to stand staring in blank surprise.

"The paper—are you sure you left it here, Don?" he asked, stooping to search the deck beneath. "I'd swear you didn't pick it up again!"

With a puzzled exclamation, Don Winslow joined him in a hunt for the missing letter.

Every scrap of paper on the desk was examined; every inch of the desk's interior was covered. Don's own pockets were turned inside out. Frowning, Don turned to Michael Splendor, who had been watching them in silence.

"It seems to have vanished!" he declared helplessly.

"That letter just isn't here; and yet, there's no place it could have gone. . . ."

"Don't be too sure, Commander!" said the cripple, calmly pointing to the half-open door. "It *could* have gone that way, with no more trouble than a sneak thief would take to lift it. There were several minutes, ye mind, when none of us was watching that side of the cabin. 'Tis me own fault, for I should have been on guard. Not even a Government vessel is safe from Scorpion spies!"

V

STRUCK DOWN FROM BEHIND

Like a picture ship on a blue enameled sea, the gunboat *Gatoon* steamed quietly on her way. Not even a ground swell disturbed the level of her white decks, or raised an extra dash of spray from her cutwater.

Yet storm and violence, in human form, were already aboard her. Within the vessel's narrow confines, loyal officers and citizens of a great nation were pitted against the unknown agents of a fiendish power. Each side now stood on its guard, ready for the battle to open; but when or where the first blow would be struck, only the Scorpion himself could tell.

The strain of waiting was hardest, of course, upon Don and his friends, who at this moment were gathered under an awning on the *Gatoon's* after deck. They knew that one or more of Scorpia's agents were on board, disguised no doubt as members of the gunboat's enlisted crew.

They were aware that the enemy would stop at nothing—not even at destroying the ship with every living soul—if that could be accomplished. Yet they were helpless to do a thing until trouble showed itself in visible form.

Don Winslow, standing by the after rail, had just

finished telling about the spy he had almost caught listening at his cabin door. That incident fitted perfectly with the theft of Michael Splendor's decoded letter. Unfortunately, the brief glimpse Don had had of the skulker was not enough to identify him.

"All I saw," he admitted, in response to Captain Riggs' query, "was a man's white clad arm and shoulder disappearing around the corner of the bulkhead. It didn't look like a seaman's blouse!"

"You mean, it might have been an officer's, Don?" cried Mercedes Colby, leaning forward in her deck chair.

"Or a petty officer's or even a cabin steward's," responded the young commander. "That really isn't much to go on in naming a suspect, you see."

"I'm sure, Winslow," said Captain Riggs stiffly, "that every commissioned officer here aboard is above suspicion. As for the enlisted personnel, of course, I can't be sure. There were some replacements made in the crew before we shoved off from Guantanamo, and a spy might have come aboard with them. About the only thing we can do is to check their enlistment records."

"The very idea I was about to suggest!" agreed Michael Splendor. "Suppose you and Commander Winslow look through the papers now, Captain, and let us know what you find. Meantime, Lieutenant Pennington and I will try to entertain Miss Colby. We'll meet again at mess, this evening, if nothing happens before then."

When Don and the captain had gone below, the man in the wheel chair turned his keen blue eyes on the two young people beside him.

"Sometimes, me friends," he said earnestly, "I have a hunch that some great thing is going to happen. And happen it does, despite every circumstance against it. In this case me hunch is that the Scorpion's power will be broken, and himself a prisoner, six months from this very day!"

A low whistle from Red Pennington greeted Splendor's statement.

"But those were almost my own words to Don this morning!" the stocky lieutenant exclaimed. "Thanks to Don Winslow, we've matched every move the enemy has made with a better one. The Scorpion must be desperate, right now. And desperation usually goes before a flop, doesn't it?"

"Very often, it does," replied Michael Splendor cautiously. "But I'm afraid the Scorpion is more angry than desperate at this moment, for all the damage we have done him. 'Tis rather because of that code letter, and the opening it gives us, that I'm so hopeful of success. As you recall, it tells us there is to be a meeting of Scorpia members in San Francisco, with Cho-San himself in charge!"

"And who," asked Mercedes Colby, as Splendor paused, "is this person you call Cho-San?"

Once more a look of gloomy absorption had spread across the crippled man's features. His eyes, gazing outboard upon the sunlit Caribbean, had the look of a sleepwalker's.

"Cho-San," he murmured, "is a chosen member of the inner circle of Scorpia. It was he and his evil master, the Scorpion, who made me the cripple I am today. 'Twas their devilish torture, in the chamber of horrors they call the Dragon Room. . . ."

A shudder gripped the big, helpless body of Michael Splendor, cutting off his strange speech. When it had passed, he sighed and blinked rapidly, like a man awaking from a nightmare.

"What was I speaking about? Ah, yes, I remember!" he said in a stronger voice. "Cho-San is the Scorpion agent in charge of all war-provoking operations from San Francisco to Singapore. Any meeting which he calls among Scorpia's members is of the utmost importance. It means a fresh attempt to stir up war among civilized nations, so that, from the wreckage of human lives and fortunes, the Scorpion may pick more blood-stained wealth and power. The Naval Intelligence knows all that, but we need legal evidence before we can trap the archcriminal."

"I see what you mean now, sir!" put in Red excitedly. "You're hoping that Don Winslow may be able to horn in on that secret meeting in some way. If he could do that, he'd get the evidence you need!"

At Splendor's nod of assent, Mercedes Colby caught her breath sharply.

"But wouldn't such an attempt be horribly danger-ous?" she protested. "Just supposing they caught Don eavesdropping, or present in disguise—what chance would he have of getting out alive?"

"Very little, I am afraid," replied the man in the wheel chair. "But remember, my dear, the United States Navy is a fighting service, where men and officers expect to risk their lives in the cause of peace. Look! Here comes Captain Riggs, and he seems to be in a hurry. Perhaps he has news. . . ."

The captain took the short ladder to the yacht's poop deck in two leaps. His expression showed both worry and anger.

"Lieutenant Pennington!" he clipped out harshly. "I'm afraid you're needed below, in my cabin. Commander Winslow. . . ."

He paused, biting his lip as if at a loss for further speech.

"Go on, sir!" prompted Red in a strained voice. "What's happened to Don? Has he been taken sick?"

"He's been attacked!" blurted Riggs. "Struck down from behind and then chloroformed. The doctor is with him now."

Red waited for no more. Forgotten were gassed lungs and wobbly knees as he plunged down the ladder and dived into the cabin country, several jumps ahead of Riggs himself.

Moments later Splendor and Mercedes Colby joined the anxious little group. Don Winslow was sitting up in the Captain's swivel chair, looking decidedly "green around the gills." The ship's doctor was binding a compress about his head; and, despite the draft through open door and skylight, the whole cabin smelled of chloroform.

"I guess you people will have to tell me what happened," the young commander was mumbling. "One minute I was looking through a pile of enlistment records—and the next, I was lying on the deck under the table, and feeling sick as a pup! What fell on me, anyhow, Doc?"

"A piece of lead pipe, to judge by the swelling," growled the medical officer. "Someone wanted to put you to sleep in a hurry, and keep you that way. He used chloroform after slugging you."

"You sure came out of it in a hurry, though, Don!" laughed Red Pennington, rather shakily. "I'd no sooner picked you up off the deck than you up and socked me in the eye!"

"I'm still slug-nutty; so you'd better watch out, Mercedes!" grinned Don, taking the glass of water the girl handed him. "But, seriously, I'd like to know who downed me, and why. Have you any idea, Captain Riggs?"

"Yes, Commander," answered the officer gloomily. "I believe it was a brutal attempt at murder by some one of the enlisted personnel. I shall do my best to hunt the scoundrel down before we reach port. Meantime, I can only blame myself for leaving you alone. If I had not returned when I did . . ."

"Don't take it that way, Captain!" protested Don Winslow, earnestly. "You weren't to blame. And as for the notion of a murder attempt—wouldn't a killer have used something surer than a blackjack and chloroform? Those things are a thief's weapons."

"Exactly, Commander!" spoke the deep voice of Michael Splendor. "Ye've named the means and the motive all in the same breath. A theft it was, to be sure; and if ye'll just glance about the place, ye'll see quick enough what the rascal stole."

A startled silence fell upon the other five persons in the cabin. It was broken when Don, struggling up from his chair, cried sharply:

"The enlistment records! They're gone, the whole stack of them!"

VI

MURDER BELOW DECKS

One mystery had been solved, but it had given rise to a more sinister problem. Michael Splendor was the one who pointed this out, as Don Winslow and his friends sat that evening at the officers' mess.

How, he asked, could the thief have known Don was making a search of the enlistment records?

There were various answers offered on the spur of the moment. Mercedes Colby suggested that Don and the captain had been overheard talking about it on their way to the cabin; but that point was quickly settled. Neither man had mentioned it before reaching Riggs' cabin.

Red's answer was that the thief had happened to see Don through the open door, as he sat at the captain's table. This sounded reasonable, until Michael Splendor told them he had tried looking through the door. From outside the cabin, he stated, neither table nor record file could be seen.

"The conclusion is, me friends," he said with a troubled frown, "that the man who struck down Commander Winslow knew in advance what he was going to do, and why. He had time to plan the job, and wait for his chance to catch his victim alone. *He knew the very moment we decided to search those records for a clue!"*

In the shocked silence which followed Splendor's words, Riggs pushed back his chair. The captain's face had the look of a man just charged with murder.

"In other words, you accuse me, Mr. Splendor!" he said hoarsely, rising to his feet. "By George, sir! If you were not a cripple, I would . . ."

"Please, Captain Riggs!" the voice of Michael Splendor rang sharp as a trumpet call. "I am accusing no one of us—least of all yourself. Now, look me in the eye and smile, me friend; for in faith I would sooner accuse meself than anyone in this cabin!"

Slowly the color came back into Captain Riggs' cheeks. Sinking back into his chair at the head of the table, he did his best to smile, though it was a hard attempt.

"I believe you, Mr. Splendor!" he said huskily. "But the way you put the evidence gave me an ugly start, sir. It seemed to point to me alone as the attacker, or at least as the one person whose whereabouts were unaccounted for at the time of the attack on Winslow."

"Indeed it did, Captain," admitted the man in the wheel chair, apologetically, "and sorry I am for not choosing me words more carefully! I was just tryin' to show all of ye how closely we are being spied upon. I meself could have sworn that no one was in earshot of our party this afternoon. Yet our every speech was heard and noted by the enemy. Our future plans must be told in whispers behind locked doors, I fancy."

Throughout the rest of the meal there was a lively argument about dictaphones and other means of eavesdropping which the spy might have used. It all proved highly amusing to the Scorpion spy, who was listening in on every word, by the aid of a clever electrical "ear."

Small and easily concealed as a man's wrist watch, the device was a powerful amplifier of ordinary sounds. These were transmitted over threadlike wires to a earphone, palmed in the spy's hand.

Turned toward a ship's ventilator or porthole, or toward a party conversing on deck, the mechanical "ear" could pick up even whispered speech without the slightest difficulty.

But while this comparatively harmless eavesdropping was in progress, a far more sinister drama was being enacted below decks. It was the old, old game of death, which has been played since life began upon the earth, and the first killer stalked his unsuspecting prey.

Deep in the bowels of the ship, amid the click and whir of oiled machinery, Chief Petty Officer Ahern began his evening watch. He was a man of about thirty years, with a well-muscled body, and keen, blue Irish eyes. In six years he had risen from Fireman Second Class to Chief Machinist's Mate.

At the moment, Ahern was the only man in the engine room of the *Gatoon*. Lieutenant Allen, the Engineer Officer, was in his own stateroom, cleaning up for the evening meal. The other Machinist's Mates were off watch. The nearest members of the "black gang" were sweating in the boiler room, forward.

Ahern was whistling an old Irish ditty as he moved about, checking the smoothly running machinery. Thought of danger was the farthest thing from his mind as he paused to glance up at the stars shining through the fiddley hatch above his head.

All at once his body stiffened as if in agony. His hands clawed at his throat. Mouth open and eyes popping from their sockets, he reeled backward in a grotesque dance of death.

As he fell, struggling, to the iron deck, a man in ordinary seaman's uniform dodged past him toward the main steam line. There was a quick sharp hammering; a hiss of escaping steam. Then the seaman reappeared, his features covered by a white handkerchief.

Briefly he stooped over Ahern's limp body, fumbling at the swollen, purple neck. The next moment, swift as a startled rat, he slipped out of sight behind a bulkhead.

Five minutes later, Lieutenant Allen came on deck for a breath of air before going to mess. Glancing toward the fiddley hatch, he noticed a wisp of steamy vapor rising from it. In alarm he sprang forward to look below. The heavy reek of hot engine oil met his nostrils as he bent over the hatch. The hum and clink of smoothly moving metal rose with it to reassure him. Only the steamy mist between decks, and a slowing of the engine's rhythmic beat spelled danger to the officer.

Turning to the engine room ladder, Lieutenant Allen made the lower deck in record time. Through a mist of steam, he made out the body of the Chief Machinist's Mate. Pausing beside it only long enough to read the signs of death, he pressed on as far as he dared toward the broken steam line.

Up on the *Gatoon's* bridge, Lieutenant Darnley caught the engine room's urgent signal. Picking up the speaking tube, he barked a short acknowledgement.

"Allen speaking," came the terse reply. "Inform Captain Riggs of attempt to sabotage the ship's engines. Chief Machinist's Mate Ahern is dead at his post. Must stop engines and pull boiler fires at once."

The meal was just over in the officers' mess. With a low exclamation Don Winslow jumped up and stepped to the nearest porthole.

"If I'm not mistaken, Captain," he said, turning to face the others, "this ship is losing way. The engines, . . . hear that, sir? The vibration has stopped completely!"

Captain Riggs sprang to his feet, scowling.

"You're right, Commander!" he cried. "We'll be losing steerage way in a few moments. I'll ring the bridge and find out. . . ."

A heavy knocking on the cabin door interrupted. Opening it, the captain faced a breathless yeoman, whose message of disaster fairly tumbled from his lips.

"Trouble with the main steam line, sir!" the enlisted man reported. "And the Chief Machinist's Mate has met with an accident, too. Lieutenant Allen requests your presence at once in the engine room!"

VII

"MAN OVERBOARD!"

Shoulder to shoulder with Captain Riggs, Don Winslow made for the engine room ladder. In their wake hurried the medical officer and Lieutenant Red Pennington. Mercedes, at Michael Splendor's insistence, stayed behind in the cabin.

Not one of them believed that the "accidents" reported by the yeoman were at all accidental. With Scorpion spies aboard trouble could be expected from any quarter. Unfortunately, there was no guessing in advance where disaster would break out; or treachery, for that matter. Even as the *Gatoon's* afterguard was bending over Ahern's twisted corpse in the engine room, a shadowy form slipped into the radio shack, abaft the galley. In the faint glow of a shaded bulb, the man's face was a mere blur. Only his hands showed in dark outline, as they fingered a pair of invisible dials.

Abruptly the fellow sat down, his right hand now concealed beneath the table. A faint, almost inaudible clicking began spelling out in International Morse Code: 'SCP—SCP—Acknowledge—SPC—SPC . . ."

Almost immediately came the reply—a hoarse, murmuring voice from outer space: *"Go ahead SC-3 with your report."*

Again the faint ticking filled the tiny room.

"Orders carried out," it spelled rapidly. "Engines disabled for the next twenty-four hours. CS-3."

There was silence for a full minute. Then the voice in the radiophone breathed harshly: "The master is pleased. Stand by at midnight for further instructions. That is all."

Below decks the *Gatoon's* medical officer rose, white-faced, from his examination of the Chief Machinist's Mate.

"This man is dead, though the body is still quite warm!" he stated. "I should say he had been strangled by a noose of thin wire, which became embedded in the flesh. Somebody removed the thing before we got here."

Lieutenant Allen, catching the captain's glance of query, shook his head.

"I didn't touch Ahern, except to turn him over, sir," he declared. "And there was no one else in the engine room when I arrived. Strange way to kill a man, with a wire noose!"

"The French call it *'La Garrote,'*" observed Don Winslow, stooping to pick a peculiar metal object from a dark corner of the deck. "If I'm not mistaken, this thing is it! Looks as if the killer dropped it in his hurry to get away."

At his words the others turned to stare in fascinated horror. The death instrument was a loop of extremely thin but tough steel wire, threaded through a small metal hand grip. A sharp pull on the latter tightened and locked the strangling noose in the same motion.

"See!" remarked the young Intelligence Officer. "A man could hide this weapon in his closed hand, or slip it into a watch pocket. It's deadlier than a knife in the back. Look here, Captain! No need to let the crew know just how Ahern was killed, is there? A thing like this could demoralize a ship's company in no time!"

The grizzled ship's master met Don's look in thoughtful silence.

"I understand, Commander," he said at last. "Knowing what *we* do, every enlisted man aboard would be suspecting his mates—afraid to turn his back for a second, for fear of feeling his wind shut off! You're right about keeping it quiet. We'll put poor Ahern in the bos'n's locker, and take the key away. Then the engine crew can get busy at that broken steam line. . . . How long before we can get under way again, Lieutenant?"

Lieutenant Allen shook his head.

"If it were only the steam line, I'd say four or five hours, sir," he replied dubiously. "But I saw what looked like emery dust near the main shaft bearings. If any of that stuff's been used we might not make port for a week, if then. All depends on what we find in the next hour, sir!"

"And on how close a watch we keep after that, Captain!" put in Don Winslow. "I'd suggest an armed guard be stationed at every vital part of this ship. Lieutenant Pennington and I will help you keep watch topside, sir."

Tossing a wink over his shoulder to Red, he turned to the ladder leading on deck.

Sometime after midnight the two young officers stood shoulder to shoulder in the shadow of a port lifeboat, the wind blowing their whispered words out to sea.

"Got your automatic handy, Red?" Don asked casually, resting an arm on the ship's rail. "We're part of that guard I mentioned to Captain Riggs, you know. The difference is that we're not stationed anywhere in particular."

"I cleaned and loaded my gun before mess gear blew this evening," young Pennington answered. "But, say! Do you really think there'll be another attempt to put the *Gatoon* out of commission?"

"I do," Don replied, "though mere sabotage wouldn't be the Scorpion's real object. He doesn't go in for small-time stuff. He'd like to sink us all without a trace, and if I didn't know that we'd destroyed his pirate submarine . . ."

"But maybe he's got another we don't know about!" cut in Red excitedly. "With her engines crippled, this old cutter'd be an easy mark for a torpedo. Or for any armed yacht the Scorpion might have handy. Say, Don, I'll bet that's the answer!"

"Keep your shirt on, Red!" Don Winslow laughed softly. "Your theory sounds okay, if you say it fast, but don't let it scare you off on a wrong tack. I'd stake my commission on there *not* being another enemy submarine in these waters; and as for an armed yacht attacking us—well, the *Gatoon's* guns outrange any but a destroyer's. No! There's some worse danger afloat, and it's up to us . . ."

Don's words trailed off into silence. Stepping deeper into the lifeboat's shadow, his form was suddenly blotted out.

"Red!" came his low call, above the slosh of waves against the ship's side.

At once, the stocky lieutenant moved in the direction of Don's voice. Feeling his way along the lifeboat's keel, he felt his arm grasped firmly. An instant later an end of light cordage was pressed into his hand.

"That's the second I've located," Don Winslow whispered in his friend's ear. "My hand happened to find the first one by accident. What do you make of it?"

"Why—it's a boat lashing, Don!" muttered Red, wonderingly. "That means the tarpaulin's loose, and a stiff breeze would lift it. . . . Huh! You don't suppose that's where the killer's hiding himself—right in this boat above our heads?"

"He may have hidden *anything!*" Don answered briefly. "Here, let me stand on your shoulders and take a look!"

As Red braced himself, Don went up, catlike, to grip the lifeboat's gunwhale. Fishing in a pocket, he produced a small flashlight. It's beam, thrust under the canvas boat cover, lighted up the whole cavelike space beneath.

Red, crouched in the darkness below, felt Don's weight suddenly leave his shoulders. Glancing up, he saw his friend's dim form disappearing inside the boat.

Moments passed, with only a faint whisper of movement from inside the covered lifeboat. Red Pennington waited nervously at his post, alert for the slightest sound of approaching footsteps. If the spy had hidden something of value, the fellow might be coming back for it at any time!

Red's reasoning was better than his hearing, as a matter of fact. When he did hear the faint step behind him, it was too late to turn. Jerking his head to one side, the stocky lieutenant just saved himself.

A numbing blow descended on his shoulder. With a grunt, Red whirled, his fist coming up in a wicked hook which contacted flesh and bone. The unseen assailant's gasp of pain came a second before Red's whoop: "I've got him, Don! Come—ugh!"

The thug's elbow jammed into Red's midriff, and loosened a perfectly good hammer lock. The lieutenant gagged, lost his grip and his footing together, as the enemy tripped him with a jiu-jitsu trick.

At that second, Don Winslow's lithe form dropped from above.

Only darkness and the snakelike agility of the Scorpion spy prevented his capture then and there. The man leaped over Red's body, barely avoiding Don's rush, and jumped for the rail beyond the lifeboat.

Red, scrambling to his feet, lunged for the boat's forward end. Without warning there came a heavy splash from overside. Don's shout, "Man overboard!" followed instantly.

"G-great guns, Don!" Red gulped, bringing up against the rail. "I thought he'd knocked *you* overside! What happened, anyway?"

"He jumped!" clipped Don Winslow as other voices on deck and bridge took up the cry of *"Man overboard!"* "Listen, Red! You hustle aft and get a place in the first boat that's lowered. Don't tell 'em the whole story—only that someone attacked you and jumped overboard when you fought back. Lively now, before anybody sees us together!"

Badly mystified, Red Pennington trotted aft to the group gathering around Number Three lifeboat. He had a hundred questions to ask, starting with: Why was Don staying behind? On the other hand, orders were orders, and questions would keep until Don chose to answer them.

VIII

THE SECOND ATTACK

Sixty seconds from the moment Don shouted warning, Number Three lifeboat was swinging, fully manned, from her davits. On the dark water below, two life preservers, with patent flares attached, floated along the *Gatoon's* portside. The ship, with engines dead, rolled gently in the trough of a gentle ground swell.

For a rescue at night, no better conditions could be asked. The trouble was that, from the moment Red Pennington's attacker had hit the water, there had been no sign of him. No second splash or cry for help had been heard.

Was the fellow a suicide—deliberately drowning in preference to being caught? Or had he just gone down, unable to swim?

One guess was as good as another. Except that the man was a Scorpion agent, Don Winslow would have given the fellow up for lost. As it was, he suspected a trick.

Thinking back, he recalled that the spy had not hit the water all sprawled out like a man who had lost his balance. There had been only the single, clean *plunk* of an expert dive.

But where, in mid-ocean, could the man have swum? To a waiting boat, somewhere out of sight in the darkness?

There was one more alternative. As the idea flashed across Don's brain, he whirled and ran to the starboard rail. After sweeping the ship's side in one quick glance, he turned again and darted back to the after deck.

Halted at the taffrail, the young officer leaned far over, his eyes squinting to pierce the darkness under the gunboat's stern. After a moment, he straightened up with a satisfied nod, and strode back to the portside.

A little group of ship's officers stood beside Mercedes and Michael Splendor near the davits, just as Don approached. All of them caught the young commander's quiet words.

"Send your boat around under the stern, Captain Riggs," Don Winslow murmured. "Our man is there, clinging to the rudder post. If we go softly, we can all get back to the taffrail in time to see the fun!"

For an instant Riggs stared in unbelief, then turned to snap an order at the men below. As the oars resumed their steady stroke alongside, Don led his friends aft on tiptoe. He knew the questions they wanted to ask; but there was no time now for talk.

A few feet from the taffrail, Don signaled the two ship's officers to stand by. He himself stooped with one hand on the line of the taffrail log.

The wait was not long. As the lifeboat started to round the stern, the stout line under Don's fingers jerked taut. By its motion he knew that his man was climbing, hand over hand.

Only a trained athlete could have performed such a feat, for the line was barely thick enough to hold a man's weight. The climber's hands must have been cut raw after the first half dozen grips, but he came doggedly on. At the last moment before his head appeared, Don drew back in a wrestler's crouch.

A lunge, a harsh oath, a brief, desperate struggle, and it was over. The unknown, who had attacked Red Pennington and then plunged into the sea, now stood on deck, panting in the grip of three strong men.

"So what?" he demanded insolently. "Now ya got me, wot ya gonna do with me? I ain't done nothin' wrong. A guy up an' slugs me in the dark, an' I fall overboard, an' now ya grab me. So what!"

Don's flashlight, turned on the man's face showed a pair of small, ratty eyes set in animallike features. The fellow was desperate, and trying to cover it up with a line of bluff.

"Looks as if we'd caught our murderer, all right!" gritted Captain Riggs, after a shrewd glance. "This seaman is one of the replacements we took on in Guantanamo. Shall I throw him in the brig now, Commander, or do you wish to question him first?"

Don Winslow snapped out his light.

"The questioning had better wait, Captain," he replied quickly. "I've just discovered something that may be of vital importance to us and every honest sailor aboard. Suppose we all talk it over in your cabin, as soon as this spy is safely under lock and key!"

On his way to the captain's quarters, Don Winslow stopped by Number Three davits and waited until the lifeboat had been swung inboard with its crew. As Red Pennington stepped to the deck, the young commander seized his arm and led him back into the shadows amidships. A few quick words covered the rat-faced seaman's capture.

"And now we'll see what his game was, Red," Don whispered, moving over to the port rail. "Give me a boost up into that boat with the unlashed cover and stand by for trouble. But don't let anybody slug you from behind this time!"

"I won't, don't kid yourself!" muttered the stocky lieutenant, stooping to take Don's weight. "But, say! You must have found something up there the first time, or you wouldn't be so anxious to look again. Can't you wait long enough to tell a man . . . ?"

But Don was already over the gunwhale and inside the boat. This time several minutes passed before his head and shoulders appeared from under the tarpaulin.

"Take these, Red!" he said softly, passing down a loose packet of papers. "And put them out of sight. I'm coming down now."

Swinging light to the deck, he drew his pocket gun and led the way back aft.

"Wha-what the dickens?" muttered Red Pennington in a hoarse whisper, as he shoved the papers under his waistband.

"Enlistment records—the missing ones!" hissed Don, glancing along the shadowy decks. "They were just part of what I found in the boat. If anybody tries to take them away from you between here and the captain's quarters . . ."

WHAM! BANG!

A tongue of flame had lanced out from behind the darkened galley. In the same split second had come Don's answering shot. Without pausing the young commander leaped straight toward the source of attack.

Red, pounding at Don's heels, tugged out his pistol.

"I'll take the starboard side!" he yelped as Don darted to port.

It seemed that the enemy, whoever he was, must be trapped, or he would have to break away in full view and get shot.

Yet it was Red Pennington whom Don bumped into, just abaft the galley.

"G-gosh! I nearly shot you, Don!" gulped the stout lieutenant. "Where'n thunder did that bird go, anyway? I was sure you were he, till I got a second look!"

For answer Don seized the knob of the galley door. It flew open to reveal a dimly lighted interior, fragrant with the smell of brewing coffee. Backed up in a corner stood Johnson, the colored cook, brandishing a razorsharp meat axe.

"Stay right wheah yo' are, befo' ah scattahs you' brains!" wailed the terrified man.

Don stepped calmly across the threshold.

"It's all right, Johnson," he said, sweeping the galley

with a quick look. "Somebody shot at us just now, and we thought he might have ducked in here. Of course, you didn't see anybody?"

Johnson's meat cleaver hit the deck with a loud clang.

"Lawsy-me, C'mandah!" he quavered. "Ah sho' thought you-all was de killah. Yassah! But ah raickon he was de one dat scooted by de po'thole, right aftah de shot! Ah jes' happened ter look out . . ."

"Which way did he go?" Don snapped, turning back to the doorway.

"He was haided aft, C'mandah," answered the colored man. "Ah jes' seen somethin' white scootin' past!"

"Come on, Red!" said Don, stepping out on deck. "We'll try the radio shack. It's part of this same superstructure, and our last bet. Hope you kept an eye on it, while I was in the galley!"

"I did," answered Red. "The only door is on this side, too. Got your flashlight ready? The place looks pitch dark!"

By this time, shouts and the sound of running feet were closing in from all sides. The twin pistol shots had roused the whole ship's company.

And now, quite unintentionally, Red Pennington made a grandstand play.

Thinking only to save Don from the killer's bullets, he slammed open the radio shack door and charged through, head down, like a football tackle. There followed a yell and the thud of heavy bodies striking the deck. An instant later half a dozen men headed by Don Winslow piled into the narrow compartment.

No shots greeted their rush, though for a moment there was plenty of confusion. With some difficulty, Red Pennington was pulled off from the kicking body of his victim, who turned out to be the *Gatoon's* radio operator. The man was breathless, battered, and evidently furious beneath his show of respect for gold braid.

He gave his name as A. Corba, Electrician First Class, and he told a reasonably straight story. He had been sitting half asleep in his chair, he said, listening in to the radio conversations between other ships in the Caribbean.

Suddenly he'd heard two pistol shots, and the sound of men running. He was still wondering what it was all about, when the door burst open and two hundred pounds of fighting man landed on him. Naturally he'd tried to fight back, but his attacker, who turned out to be Lieutenant Pennington, had him licked from the start.

Don Winslow heard the story through, without a change of expression.

"Why," he asked, "did you have the deadlights screwed over the portholes. Is that customary aboard this craft?"

"Captain Riggs' orders, sir," replied the radio operator instantly. "That is, we were all warned to let no lights show our position to any passing boat."

"He's right, Commander!" spoke up the *Gatoon's*

captain, from the doorway. "I did give that order; and it strikes me that this man's account holds water. Whoever shot at you must have gotten away, at least for the time being. What puzzles me is the reason for such an attack."

"Suppose we talk that over in your quarters, sir," Don suggested, moving toward the door. "If I'm not mistaken, we're due for more surprises before the night is over!"

IX

RED NABS A SPY

Don Winslow's brief account of the two attacks on Red and himself did little to clear up the mystery which hung like a dark cloud over the *Gatoon's* after guard. Both assaults appeared to have the same object, however—to get back the stolen enlistment records which Don had found hidden in the lifeboat. For some reason the enemy was afraid to have those records examined.

"That's how I've figured it out," Don told the little company gathered in the captain's cabin, "either the records of Scorpion agents among the crew are missing, or they've been forged. In any case, a careful check should tell the story."

Spreading out the rumpled enlistment papers on the captain's table, he commenced a swift search, while Riggs and Red Pennington looked over his shoulders. All at once he picked up one of the documents and smoothed it out. The name on the outside read: "Anton Corba," with the rating noted as "Radioman, First Class."

"But why pick that one, Commander?" asked Captain Riggs sharply. "What reason have you to suspect . . ."

"Look, Captain!" Don Winslow interrupted. "The signatures on this record show signs of tracing. Forgery, all right, but a mighty clumsy job. Just study it for a minute and give me your opinion."

Handing the paper to Riggs, he whispered rapidly in the officer's ear:

"I have a hunch we are being overheard now. Corba or some other spy may be the eavesdropper. I'm sending Pennington out to check up. Meantime we must all keep talking naturally, so the fellow will not suspect."

With a nod of understanding, Riggs moved over to Michael Splendor's chair.

"I see what you mean, Commander," he said loudly. "At least one of these signatures looks smeary, but I'm no handwriting expert. Tell me what you think of it, Mr. Splendor. As chief of the Haitian Naval Intelligence, you should know about such things."

Stooping quickly, he whispered Don Winslow's plan to the cripple. At the same instant Don was muttering advice in Red's ear.

"Take off your shoes," he told the wide-eyed lieutenant. "Sneak up topside and try to locate anyone who may be eavesdropping. If you don't spot anyone, come back in five minutes. Here's my flashlight. Shove off now, and good luck! We'll carry on the show down here till you report or signal us."

As Red silently closed the cabin door behind him, he heard Michael Splendor's voice within, taking up the mock discussion. The "show" as Don called it, would be quite convincing to any eavesdropper.

And if Don was right in his guess, the spy should be easy to surprise at his work. At that hour of night, no enlisted man would have any legitimate business hanging around the cabin ventilators.

Silent as a shadow, for all his bulk, Red Pennington emerged onto the starlit deck. Slipping aft, he rounded the cabin skylight and probed the shadows under the port rail.

No glimpse of a furtive lurker rewarded him, however. With a grunt of disappointment, he padded forward, heading for the midship's superstructure.

"I'll just take a look inside the radio shack," he muttered under his breath. "Don seems to think that guy Corba's enlistment was forged—which means he may be the guy who shot at us, too. He's got a fishy mug, anyway, and his story was a little too slick when we jumped him a few minutes ago!"

The door of the radio shack was on the port side. Therefore, as an extra precaution, Red circled the superstructure to starboard, halting at the corner of the galley.

The space between the deck house and the rail was empty, yet something about it looked queer. For a moment Red stood blinking in puzzlement, trying to make out what was wrong. All at once it came to him.

The radio shack door was open at least two inches; yet no light shone through onto the white deck.

Since Navy men do not go about leaving doors ajar,

this suggested one of two things: either Corba had left in a desperate hurry, or he was still inside, *with the lights out!* Red Pennington intended to find out which.

With the utmost caution, he crept past the galley, noting that the door beyond him did not sway with the gentle roll of the ship. That meant it was propped open deliberately. But *why?*

Just as his hand was reaching for the knob, the door swung shut. Red froze in his tracks, his mind racing. Whoever had closed that two-inch opening could not have seen him. The door itself had hid his approach. The thing proved simply that the radio shack was occupied.

Before Red could plan his next move, a faint, metallic ticking caught his ear. Pressing his ear close to the shack's steel wall, he made out the familiar chatter of a wireless key, sending in International Morse Code.

"— REPORTING — EMERGENCY — ABOARD — GATOON" Red silently spelled out the message. "AGENT SC-21 SEIZED. WINSLOW AND PENNINGTON HAVE DISCOVERED FORGED ENLISTMENT PAPERS IN LIFEBOAT WE PREPARED FOR OUR GETAWAY. THIS WILL LEAD ANY MOMENT TO MY ARREST AND THAT OF AGENT SC-17. PLEASE ADVISE NEXT MOVE. SC-3."

While listening, Red Pennington had slipped Don's flashlight from his pocket. As the message ended, he wrenched open the door and shot the bright beam into the radio shack. It's spotlight steadied on the tense figure of Corba, seated beside the room's small tool bench.

"Just hold that pose, sailor!" gritted the stocky lieutenant. "No—keep your left hand under the bench! Don't move a muscle——"

Whipping out his pocket gun, Red slammed two shots at the steel decking, close to Corba's feet. Instantly the white-faced radioman froze in his chair, his pose still as a statue's.

"That's better!" clipped the lieutenant, as shouts and the stamp of feet sounded from the cabin country. "In just a moment you're going to tell your story over again; and it had better be the right one this time. Do you get me, *Agent SC-3?*"

Warned by Red's sharp call, Don Winslow halted the captain and Lieutenant Darnley outside the radio shack. Stepping inside alone, he snapped on the lights.

"Great work, Red!" he approved, when the red-haired lieutenant briefly outlined what had happened. "We've caught our eavesdropper this time, and . . ."

He broke off as a harsh whisper rose, seemingly from beneath the workbench.

"AGENT SC-3 AND SC-17, ATTENTION!" the weird voice rasped. "YOU ARE INSTRUCTED TO LEAVE THE SHIP AT ONCE, USING LIFE-BELTS. SEAPLANE WILL PICK YOU UP AT DAWN. SC-21 WILL PAY PENALTY FOR HIS FAILURE WHEN WE BOMB GATOON FROM THE AIR. THAT IS ALL!"

A gasp from the unhappy Corba gave Don Winslow

the cue for his next play. Ignoring the startled questions of Captain Riggs and Lieutenant Allen, he faced the radio operator.

"All right, Corba!" he said tightly. "That message shows you just where you get off. Like SC-21, you're going to pay the penalty for failure, when and if bombs start dropping on this vessel! Is your loyalty to Scorpia strong enough to stand up under that?"

Hollow-eyed with fear, the Scorpion spy shook his head.

"You've named it, Commander!" he said hoarsely. "The Scorpion don't have much mercy for them that are fools enough to get caught. But what good'll it do, sir, if I tell you what I know? We're all bound for Davy Jones' locker, now!"

Don Winslow's laugh rang as hard as the slap of bullets on steel armor plate.

"We *were,* maybe, but we're taking a new tack, sailor!" he barked. "Now we know what your murderous pals are up to, we can outthink and outfight them too. The only man aboard who's bound for Davy Jones is——"

"Captain!" cried a breathless voice on deck. "The prisoner, Durkin—the man you put in the brig, sir—he's dead! Hanged himself, with a loop of wire he'd made fast to a steampipe. We found this note, written on an old envelope. Here it is, sir!"

After a startled pause, Captain Riggs stepped inside to hold a crumpled envelope under the light.

"What do you make of this, Commander?" he

growled. "Things are happening a bit too fast for me to keep my bearings tonight, this note, for instance! It says: 'I queered your engines and killed the Chief Machinist's Mate. When the Scorpion strikes, you'll think I did Ahern a favor. *Signed,* Durkin.'"

"And so exit Scorpion Agent SC-21!" observed Don Winslow harshly. "He killed himself rather than go down later with the ship. That leaves one enemy agent still unidentified. Who is he, Corba?"

"Seaman Second Class, by the name of Mink," replied the radioman sullenly. "He's just a tough gorilla we brought aboard for strong arm work. As it turned out, we didn't have to use him."

"Which means *you* were the bird who shot at us tonight from the corner of the galley!" put in Red Pennington. "You sure hated to let us get a look at those forged enlistment records, didn't you, Mr. A. Corba?"

With a snort of anger, Captain Riggs turned to the door.

"The whole business smells like plain mutiny to me!" he declared. "While you're questioning this man, Commander, I'm going to hunt up Seaman Second Class Mink, and throw him in irons! Join me in my quarters, gentlemen, when you're ready to compare notes."

X

A DESPERATE SCHEME

The questioning of Anton Corba, Electrician First Class, took less than twenty minutes; but it laid bare the whole Scorpion plot to destroy the gunboat.

Corba and the other two spies had come aboard at Guantanamo. The Navy men whose places they took, had been kidnapped by other Scorpion agents, and held until the gunboat sailed.

"The rest was easy, sir," the prisoner stated, with a nervous glance at Red Pennington's gun. "I rigged up a special sending key and an extra short-wave receiver with the help of stuff I'd smuggled aboard. I kept in touch with the Scorpia headquarters by tunin' into a new wave length they gave me each day. And I listened in to any talk aboard ship with this electric 'ear' which they say the Scorpion himself invented. Here it is, if you want to look at it."

Slipping a hand inside his blouse, Corba produced the tiny amplifier and earphone. Don Winslow took it from him, with a smile.

"Clever!" he nodded, noting the hairlike wires and fine workmanship. "I suspected something like this, Red, when I sent you up on deck to look around. With his door ajar, Sparks here could get every whisper coming up the cabin ventilators. . . . Well, Corba, if that's your name, I guess that explains how you knew we were going to search the enlistment records. The minute I was alone in the Captain's quarters, you just slipped in and bopped me on the head, eh?"

"Yes, sir!" gulped the radio operator, squirming unhappily on his chair. "You see, I had to, sir. I mean, I was afraid you'd . . ."

"Stow it!" rapped Don, his tone suddenly hard. "Get down to brass tacks, and give us the rest of this program for sinking a Navy vessel on the high seas. Putting the engines out of commission was only a starter, of course. Let's hear what comes next."

Corba's black eyes slid away from the impact of Don's steely gaze.

"Why—why, there ain't no 'next,' sir," he answered, nervously. "Not until daylight, when a couple of fast bombin' planes dive outa the sky and drop about a ton of high explosive down your fiddley hatch. What happens then don't need no imagination to figure out, sir! And no man aboard can do a thing to prevent it."

"Horse feathers!" burst out Red Pennington. "We've got anti-aircraft guns, mounted fore and aft, that can blow half a dozen fast bombers clean out of the ozone. What're you trying to do, punk? Throw a scare into us?"

Drawn-faced, the radio operator shook his head. For a second, he seemed about to reply, but instead merely licked his lips and looked away.

Don Winslow sensed that the man was half-crazy

with terror, every time he thought or spoke of the coming air attack. And for that fear there could be only one good reason.

"You might as well tell it straight, Corba!" he told the fidgeting prisoner. "Go on and admit that the ship's guns have been damaged, as well as the engines! Unable to fight or run, this ship will be just a helpless target—or so you believe. Is that it?"

The radioman's jaw dropped. He nodded weakly.

"I don't see how you guessed it, sir," he whimpered; "Mink fixed every gun two nights ago. He used an explosive metal plug that'll make the gun blow up the first time it's fired. I'd have told you before, only there ain't a thing you can do to fix 'em, sir. We're gonna be sunk, with all hands, and that's all there is to it!"

"Great jumpin' catfish!" gurgled Red Pennington. "I never thought once about the guns being jimmied too! What can we do now, Don?"

"First put this man in the brig with his gorilla shipmate!" clipped out the young commander. "After that, we're going to move a lot farther and faster than the Scorpion expects. You stay by the radio until I send up a regular guard, Red. And, Corba! March yourself straight through that door and forward to the brig. Lively now! My gun will be right at your back the whole way!"

Back in the radio shack, after seeing the lock turned on both Scorpion spies, Don Winslow sat down to compose a code radiogram to Navy Intelligence Headquarters at Washington. A trusted boatswain's mate armed with rifle and bayonet stood outside to guard against interruptions.

The message, as Red Pennington translated it aloud, read: "GATOON SABOTAGED. STOP. NOW DRIFTING OFF THE COAST OF HAITI WITH GUNS AND ENGINES DISABLED. STOP. EXPECT ATTACK BY ENEMY BOMBERS AT DAYLIGHT. STOP. SEND FAST ATTACK PLANES TO OUR ASSISTANCE AT ONCE. STOP. OUR POSITION IS . . ."

"Here's what I make it, Winslow!" interrupted Captain Riggs entering the room with sextant in one hand and a sheet of penciled figures in the other. "Good thing it's a clear night, for 'shooting' the stars. By my reckoning, we're just ten miles off the coast, and ninety more from Port-au-Prince."

"Thank you, Captain!" said Don, glancing at the other's notes. "Shall I sign your name now to this radio message? If we send it at once, those Navy planes will have barely time to get here before the fun starts!"

"Sign it yourself, Commander," replied Riggs quickly. "Your name will carry twice the weight of mine with Washington. But, blow me under if I like this idea of lying here useless till help comes! Isn't there any trick we can work out to defend ourselves with?"

"I think there is, Captain," answered Don Winslow, rising from his chair. "I'd like to talk it over first, though, with Michael Splendor. Suppose we join him, below, while Pennington is sending this radio I've just coded. Red's an expert operator, so there won't be any mistakes!"

Below, in the captain's quarters, Lieutenant Darnley had just finished outlining the situation to Splendor and Mercedes Colby. The girl was taking the latest news of sabotage and sudden death with cool courage, as became the daughter of a Navy Admiral. Even the likelihood of being bombed and sunk by a Scorpion airship failed to terrify her.

"Now that I know the worst, I'm not scared at all," she smiled pluckily. "It was *not* knowing what fiendish thing the Scorpion was planning, that was the hardest to bear. There are lots of worse deaths than drowning. And anyhow, I can't believe it will come to that!"

"Neither can I!" put in Michael Splendor, quietly. "With Don Winslow on deck, our chances of making port are better than the enemy's. He'll find a way to fight back, never fear! Besides, there's me ôwn seaplane we took aboard last night. She has two machine guns and——"

Without knocking, Captain Riggs flung open the door and entered, with Don Winslow at his heels.

"I have a few plans to talk over with you, sir!" the latter announced, halting before the cripple's wheel chair. "Lieutenant Darnley has told you the latest trouble, I suppose—about our anti-aircraft guns being jimmied?"

"He has that!" replied Splendor. "And I knew you'd have a plan to overcome that difficulty, Commander.

'Tis honored I am that ye wish to discuss it with a useless old man like me!"

"You've been called 'the brains of the Haitian Intelligence Service,'" Don retorted. "And if brains are useless, it's news to me! Joking aside, sir, there are three good reasons against our being bombed and sunk at daylight. I'll name them over, and see if you agree with me. Perhaps Captain Riggs and Lieutenant Darnley may have some valuable suggestions to make, too."

"Go ahead, Commander!" nodded the crippled man, as the others grouped themselves closer about Don. "I had a couple of scheme's in me own mind, but three sounds better yet!"

In short, rapid sentences, Don Winslow outlined the hopes of the *Gatoon's* company.

First was the message now being radioed by Red Pennington to Captain Holding of the Naval Intelligence in Washington. A squadron of light bombing planes would be taking off within an hour to come to the *Gatoon's* rescue.

Whether or not they would arrive in time was another question, of course. The distance of the nearest fighting ships, the weather they might meet on the way, and various other difficulties made the answer uncertain. Less than three hours now remained before daybreak and the Scorpion's attack.

Pursuit type planes, Don explained, could have made the distance quicker, but could not carry enough gas for a round trip.

Don's second plan was for Panama and an expert

machine gunner to take Splendor's armed seaplane up at crack of dawn to watch for enemy aircraft, and fight them off. Even if hopelessly outnumbered, the pilot and his gunner could delay an attack upon the *Gatoon*.

"And that," boomed Michael Splendor, his eyes gleaming eagerly, "is the very job I picked for meself! I'll need no legs to use a machine gun, ye see. I've already talked it over with my pilot. The lad is anxious to try his luck in a real air fight, whatever the odds. And now, Commander, let's have your third scheme. I've no doubt it includes yourself, and that redheaded lieutenant. If so, it will be the most dangerous job of all, and the most difficult, too."

"I'm not so sure of that, sir," Don protested. "In fact it's as simple as jumping overboard with a life preserver on. That's what the Scorpion's gang expect their two spies to do; so what's to keep Red and me from taking their places?"

"And then what, Don?" asked Mercedes Colby in a strained tone. "I suppose you think a Scorpion pilot will pick you up without asking questions or bothering to recognize you? More likely he'll turn his machine gun on you and leave you for the fishes. Oh, Don, don't try anything so desperately foolish!"

XI

JAWS OF DEATH

It was Michael Splendor whose reasoning finally calmed the girl's worst fears for Don and Red. It was a known rule of "Scorpia," he pointed out, that only agents who had to work in close contact should know each other, even by sight. Therefore, dressed in seamen's uniforms, the two young officers would run little risk of discovery until they actually boarded the pick-up plane.

After that, things would begin to happen fast, with probably fatal results to someone!

"You see, Mercedes," Don added, "we've simply got to capture that enemy ship! It's bound to be armed with one or more machine guns. In any case, it would double our chances of beating off enemy bombers until our own squadron shows up. And, by the way—we've got just two hours now to sunrise. We'd better get started without any more delay!"

Returning on deck, the officers found Red Pennington just signing off a code conversation with Captain Holding in Washington. The Intelligence Officer had been routed out of bed and was personally directing the despatch of fighting planes to the *Gatoon's* rescue.

It seemed doubtful, however, that the squadron could arrive in less than three hours.

"We can only hope," Captain Riggs remarked, anxiously, "that something will delay the enemy's arrival, too. The best I can do aboard is to muster the crew on deck with loaded rifles. If the bombers try diving at us, our bullets *might* take effect."

After a brief discussion, it was decided to take Don and Red in one of the lifeboats, about half a mile to leeward of the *Gatoon,* and there drop them overside. The water was fairly warm off the coast of Haiti. The only real danger they would face, while drifting about on the black, mile-deep water, would be from sharks.

The question of uniforms was quickly settled, by new outfits drawn from the ship's "slop-chest." Don was to impersonate Corba, with the red and white rating badge on his blouse sleeve placing him as a Radioman, First Class. Red, being husky and heavily built, would take the part of the "gorilla" seaman, Mink.

The change of clothing was quickly made; but first, both young officers strapped on pistol holsters under their blouses. The weapons themselves, fully loaded, were sealed in watertight oiled silk. Life belts, clumsy but buoyant, made their outfit complete.

Just before they took their places in the ready lifeboat, Lieutenant Allen came hurrying from the engine room to report a piece of good luck.

"We've repaired the steam line, sir," he said, approaching Captain Riggs, "and we had an easier job of cleaning out that emery dust from the machinery than

I had expected. We'll be ready to get under way in half an hour."

"Splendid! Great work, Lieutenant!" cried the *Gatoon's* skipper. "That gives us an extra chance in case we are bombed. A ship steaming in zigzag is a harder target to hit. We'll just drift until daylight; but see that you have full steam up by then!"

"Before then, if you don't mind, Captain!" put in Michael Splendor, rolling his wheel chair up to the rail. "The steam winch will be needed to lower yon seaplane overside. 'Tis a heavy weight to handle by manpower alone."

Captain Riggs muttered a brief consent, and turned to grip the hands of the two departing officers. Quickly, Mercedes, Splendor, and the *Gatoon's* afterguard followed suit. There were no formal good-bys; but the words spoken were packed with meaning:—

"Good luck, Don! So long, Red!"

"See you later, Commander!"

Expertly manned, the lifeboats touched the water with scarcely a sound. The boat falls were quickly released; strong arms pushed the little craft clear of the *Gatoon's* looming side. Above, the dim blur of faces at the ship's rail faded from sight.

"Out . . . oars!"

The coxswain's low spoken order came from the lifeboat's stern sheets. It was answered by the soft thudding of oars into rowlocks. Don and Red, in their seamen's uniforms, each gripped one of the long ash blades, "feathered" it by a drop of their wrists, and held it poised above the black water.

"Altogether. . . . Give way!"

At the coxswain's word, six tough muscled bodies tensed; six oar blades hit the water at the same precise instant. The little craft leaped forward like a startled fish.

Steering only by the light wind astern, it covered the half mile to leeward of the *Gatoon* in about five minutes. As there was no moon the ship could not be seen. Only the starshine, reflected from the ocean's heaving surface, showed where water ended and air began.

To a landsman, it would have given a queer sensation; adrift in a small boat at night, with nothing to see but starshine above or below; to know that a mile beneath that black water lay the hills and valleys of the ocean's bottom; to think that, in just a minute, one would be *in* that water up to one's neck, with the lifeboat pulling away, out of sight and sound!

Even the seasoned sailors in the boat with Don and Red must have had some such thoughts, though Navy discipline kept them from saying anything. When the two young officers stood up in their life belts, ready to bail out, the coxswain alone spoke up.

"Is there anything else, Commander?" he asked huskily. "Sure you don't want us to stand by for a while after you and the lieutenant go overboard?"

"Of course not, Coxswain!" replied Don with a quiet laugh. "This isn't a sea burial. It's just a job Lieutenant Pennington and I have to do. You'll probably be in more danger aboard the *Gatoon* than we will be here. Steady, now! We're going over the bow."

"Aye-aye, sir!" answered the petty officer, with a catch in his voice. "And here's wishin' you and the Lieutenant good luck!"

The lifeboat pitched and swung off as two heavy splashes sounded over her bow.

"Good luck to you, Coxs'n!" sputtered Red Pennington from the water. "Sheer off now and head for the ship! They're showing a signal light to give you your bearings."

When the last faint splash of oars faded out, Don Winslow spoke.

"Feel lonesome, Red?"

A gasping breath from the darkness gave evidence of Red's position, even before he answered.

"G-gee, Don!" he stuttered. "I wondered for a minute if you'd drifted out of hearing. Sound off again, Skipper, so I can paddle closer! I'd certainly hate to float around here in the darkness and know I was all alone. . . . Say, where are you, anyhow?"

"Here!" answered Don, shortly.

"Huh? Where? I thought you were over *there!*" burbled Red Pennington between frantic splashings. "Are you swimmin' circles around me, Skipper, or is it the darkness? Dawggone. . . ."

"It's your life preserver, Red!" Don chuckled. "Don't try to swim fast in that thing, or you'll just spin round and round. Paddle over here slowly, and I'll pass you an end of marline I brought along to lash us together."

There was some more splashing, and a final grunt of relief as Red found Don's hand holding the length of tarred cord. For a while neither of them spoke. The feeling of being suspended in wet, black space rather dampened the wish to talk.

An hour passed in gloomy, uncomfortable silence, before the first hint of daylight showed across the tossing wave tops. Little by little the night sky paled, making the water look all the blacker by contrast. Then, a mile to windward, the two officers made out the ship they had left—a faint, gray shadow breaking a wave-notched horizon.

"We've drifted quite a distance, shipmate," Don observed, gazing toward the *Gatoon*. "Too far for anybody on board to sight us! I suppose they're wondering whether or not the sharks have gotten us by now."

"What *I'm* wondering is whether that Scorpion seaplane is going to spot us or not," responded Red Pennington. "And something else just occurred to me— Will the pilot have orders to pick us up before or *after* they try the bomb the *Gatoon?* We didn't think to ask Corba that one, did we?"

"He might not have known, anyhow," Don shrugged. "Quit thinking up so many different kinds of hard luck, Red, and tell me how your appetite is. I've got some chocolate and a couple of sea biscuits stowed away in a waterproof envelope. There's no telling whether we'll eat breakfast today. . . ."

"Or be eaten *for* breakfast!" Red cut in with a yell. "Look! Isn't that a shark?"

XII

TIGERS OF THE SEA

One glance at the black, triangular fin slicing through the water was enough. It was a shark of the man-eating variety.

"Get out your gun, Red!" barked Don Winslow, reaching for his own weapon. "Hold it ready, but don't use it until the last possible moment. The smell of blood —even shark's blood—will drive the other sharks mad!"

Biting his lips, the stocky lieutenant ripped the waterproof silk from his Navy Colt's revolver. Though he could have led a landing party in the face of machine gun fire, without a qualm of fear, the idea of becoming shark meat while still alive was hard for Red Pennington to get used to.

"Here's hopin' there aren't any other sharks around!" he gulped. "If I don't see any in the next two minutes, I'm gonna shoot this one so full of holes . . ."

"Hold it!" Don Winslow rapped out. "I see another fin—no, it's three more! And more coming, off there to port. Great guns, Red! We're right in the middle of a school of them!"

Calmly, he took a squint at the chambers of his revolver making sure they were all loaded.

"You see now, Red, why I wouldn't take automatic pistols," he said. "Those things jam up after a little exposure to salt water. These revolvers can take it."

"Yeah!" responded Red bitterly. "But what good's all that goin' to do us if they come too fast for us to shoot? HEY! LOOK OUT! HE'S COMING FOR YOU, DON!"

Twenty feet to starboard, a huge fin was driving straight toward them. In another second the killer shark would roll over for the bite, Don knew.

Instead of firing, however, he brought both arms down flat on the water, with a tremendous splash. At the same time, he yelled like a trapped hyena.

With a quick swirl, the shark changed his course; but even so, it was a close call. So close that the killer's mighty tail slapped against Don's legs with numbing force.

"Wha-what's the big idea?" gurgled Red, twisting his neck to watch the shark's departure. "You had time to shoot him, Skipper!"

"But not time to stop him!" replied Don. "Anyhow, we don't want any blood in the water as near to us as that. I guess our best bet is to serve these sharks a breakfast, but keep them as far away as possible. Like this!"

Snapping up his Colt, Don Winslow fired at a circling fin, about forty yards distant. There followed the brief flurry of a wounded shark. Then, without warning, the ocean round about was lashed to a froth. Great bodies whirled and plunged in a circle of blood-stained water. From all sides, the sharp, triangular fins of the other sharks came streaking toward the center of disturbance.

"And *that*," gritted Don Winslow, "is the way they'd be bearing down on us, if I'd shot that first would-be man-eater, instead of scaring him! How'd you like to be in the middle of that ring-around-the-rosie, Red?"

"G-golly, no!" shivered the junior officer. "I've heard that sharks were cannibals; but I never thought they were such fast feeders. Look, Don! They've finished that one already. Eaten him alive!"

"In which case we'd better give them some more breakfast bacon," agreed the young commander. "Go ahead and shoot, sailor! It's your turn."

"Uh-uh, Don! It's your turn all the time," the redhead responded. "As a marksman, I'll never be in your class, and we've got to save our bullets. That way, we might keep those sea tigers busy eating themselves until the plane shows up."

Carefully Don picked his next target and fired. This time his bullet merely clipped through the shark's back fin, but the wound was enough for its blood maddened fellows. A second savage feast churned the water's surface, fifty yards away.

One by one Don's precious cartridges were expended, until only half a dozen were left. The dawn light had grown stronger now, and Red, glancing toward the distant *Gatoon,* detected movement aboard her.

"They've spotted us aboard ship!" he cried. "They're lowering a boat!"

Don Winslow's revolver cracked again.

"They'll get here just about in time," he commented. "That is, provided I don't miss any shots. Every shark in ten square miles must have smelled this party and joined it. A number of them have been looking us over, too."

"I've noticed that, Skipper, don't worry!" Red Pennington exclaimed. "It's too bad the Scorpion plane didn't get here sooner, but. . . . Say! Am I hearing things, or is that a plane's motor, over to the east?"

Above the splashing rose the snarl of an airplane motor warming up. The sound rose in pitch, then faded abruptly.

"That's Splendor and his pilot taking off!" remarked Don, his eye on the circling man-eaters. "They'll climb to ten thousand to start their watch for the bombers. Right now, I envy them!"

For a long, listening moment, there was no sound but the lapping of waves and the occasional splash of a feeding shark. Very gradually the drone of an approaching plane grew louder.

"It's not Splendor's motor," Don decided at last. "Besides, it's flying too low and straight to be on patrol. It's the Scorpion seaplane, all right, and headed straight for us!"

"It'll be here before the boat from the *Gatoon!*" cried Red Pennington. "Probably the pilot thinks the boat is after a couple of spies. If he does, he'll beat 'em to it and pick us up! Where is he, though, Don? That motor's getting close, but there's no plane in sight!"

"That's because he's flying low, right in the 'eye of

the sun,' as they say," replied the other, whipping up his gun for another shot.

The bullet missed, just as the target dived under. Another slug from Don's nearly exhausted supply furnished more living "breakfast" for the ravenous sea tigers. Two sharks swirled dangerously close to the two officers in the turmoil.

"Better start splashing and keep it up, Red!" Don Winslow advised. "Those finny devils are getting more curious about us every second. If we can keep them off just a few more minutes . . ."

CR-RASH! SLAP! SWISH!

The school of sharks scattered in all directions, as a seaplane's pontoons smashed down into the water close by.

"Ahoy, you two!" cried a voice almost over the swimmers' heads. "Climb aboard, and make it snappy! Those sharks will be back in a minute."

Looking up, Don and Red saw that a few strokes would bring them within reach of the plane's starboard pontoon. So skillfully had the pilot maneuvered his craft in the choppy waves that he was now drifting past almost within arm's reach. The man's head and arms were just visible through the cabin door which he had slid back.

Don gripped the pontoon's wet surface, heaved himself up, and reached an arm down to Red Pennington. His revolver was back in its shoulder holster, but the bulge of it was plain, he knew, under his wet blouse.

"Those sharks nearly got us at that!" he observed,

imitating Corba's whining tones. "We've been shootin' at 'em since daylight, but they was gettin' uglier every second. An' then that boat put off from the *Gatoon*. Between it and the sharks, we wouldn't have lasted five minutes longer!"

"I know all that, sailor!" snapped the pilot, glancing back at the approaching lifeboat. "Stow the gab and climb up here, so I can take off. They've got rifles in that boat!"

Muttering under his breath, the fake Corba clambered into the cabin, with his dripping companion at his heels. As they did so, the seaplane's motor burst into full-throated sound. Gracefully the ship circled, straightened out over the slapping wave tops, and took off into the wind.

"You, Mink!" called the pilot above the motor's steady roar. "They tell me you're good with a machine gun. If you want some practice, move over and man that turret piece!"

"Okay!" replied Red Pennington, taking the role of the gorilla seaman. "But wot's the idea now? We ain't gonna attack the *Gatoon* all by ourselves, are we?"

The seaplane listed steeply in a sharp bank. As it swung back toward the drifting yacht, the pilot laughed harshly.

"We're going to put a few holes in that lifeboat, just for the fun of it!" he said. "I'll give 'em a burst from the wing guns, and you finish the job as we leave 'em astern."

"This job," cut in Don Winslow's voice, "is already

finished, pilot! Ease over and give me those controls, or take a bullet through your ribs!"

The Scorpion pilot stiffened under the hard pressure of Don's gun muzzle. His lips drew back in an animal snarl.

"You're not Corba!" he grated, as the young Navy Commander pulled back on the joystick. "And this other guy isn't Mink. What's the game, anyway?"

Red Pennington's revolver prodded gently between the man's shoulder blades, as Don banked the seaplane for a fast climb.

"Just a couple of Navy lads taking over for Uncle Sam," the grinning lieutenant answered. "Your precious pals, Mink and Corba are locked up in the *Gatoon's* brig. That's where we're going to put you, if we're lucky in the coming dogfight."

XIII

WINGS OF DESTRUCTION

The Scorpion pilot sat chewing his lips in silence, while Red tied his wrists behind him. Mixed anger and admiration showed on the man's darkly handsome face.

"If you mean you're going to shoot it out with our bombers, you're a couple of suicidal nuts!" he exclaimed finally. "They'll outnumber you three to one, and they all mount one-pounder guns, firing through a hollow prop shaft. Who do you guys think you are, to buck odds like that?"

Don pushed the sturdy ship to its steepest possible climb.

"See that other plane, right above us?" he asked. "It's ours, and it's armed like this one, with guns fore and aft. The odds won't be too bad for us, when your three ships show up. And if they don't get here pretty quick they'll run into some more of the United States Navy. There's a squadron of fast attack bombers due here in half an hour."

"Which is going to be just half an hour too late!" remarked Red Pennington in a strained voice. "Here come the Scorpion bombers right on our tail! And—"

"SC-25, acknowledge!" blared a voice from the seaplane's radio. "Ahoy, Count Borg! Explain presence of second seaplane. Also, why *Gatoon* has steam up. Is anything wrong?"

Don Winslow's response was instantaneous. In a flash he realized that the question he'd heard came from the leading bomber. His hand darted to a switch just below the plane's radio dials.

"Borg speaking!" he said, in excellent imitation of his captive's voice. "Second seaplane is okay. *Gatoon* appears defenseless except for rifles on deck. Come ahead!"

Still climbing, Don Winslow's captured seaplane was already above the Scorpion ships. They were, he saw, closing up on a course that would bring them directly over the *Gatoon* at about three thousand feet. Not fearing the gunboat's crippled anti-aircraft, they were going to dive bomb—from a height that would insure direct hits!

A plan of attack grew swiftly in the young commander's mind. It would require perfect timing, and if it failed . . .

But this was not the moment to think of failure. Circling back Don headed for the first enemy ship just as it commenced its deadly bombing dive.

The seaplane's air speed mounted. Under full throttle it plunged to intercept the Scorpion bomber.

Just as a crash seemed certain, twin streams of fire ripped from Don's forward guns. In the same split second he zoomed, bringing the second and third Scorpion planes briefly in front of his sights.

On, up and over in a complete loop he flew the

snarling little ship. As yet he was unable to see the effect of his surprise attack. Had he crippled one or more of the enemy, or had his bullets missed their vital spots?

Don's answers came all in a bunch, as he leveled out, less than three thousand feet above the sea. Directly below him a heavy concussion rocked the air. White water geysered upward alongside the *Gatoon*.

The first enemy plane had pancaked, and had been blown to bits by its own bomb load. But the others?

A row of bullet holes appeared suddenly in Don's left wing surface, creeping toward the cabin. As Don zoomed, a dial on his instrument board smashed to bits.

The machine gun in the plane's after turret fired two short bursts, followed by Red Pennington's shout.

"Two of 'em, diving at us from port and starboard!" yelped the lieutenant. "They've got us bracketed—"

The sudden jerk of his safety belt cut off Red's speech, as Don threw his ship into a barrel roll. It was a desperate attempt to dodge the deadly cross-fire of the two enemy planes until he could bring his own guns to bear.

But now another ship had joined the dogfight. Michael Splendor's open seaplane, diving from ten thousand feet, unleashed a stream of bullets at the enemy.

Coming out of his roll at barely a hundred feet, Don climbed his ship in a furious effort to get back in the fight. But already the Scorpion pilots had had enough. One after another, they fluttered down like wounded birds, their wings and fuselages pierced in a hundred places.

Both managed to take the water safely, though they began to sink a moment later. Their crews plunged overboard, swimming toward the *Gatoon*.

Immediately a boat was lowered by the yacht. Glancing down Don Winslow cut his throttle.

"We'll land on the other side of the *Gatoon*, Red, and taxi in under the stern. Splendor will moor his plane near the bow until they hoist it aboard, and . . ."

"Wait, Don!" Red Pennington cried sharply. "Splendor's waggling his wings to signal us. He's trying to tell us something."

Don Winslow, banking in a slow turn squinted out over the sunlit ocean. Against the horizon, just over the tail of the other seaplane appeared a V-shaped group of dots.

"It's the Navy squadron we radioed for!" the young commander chuckled. "I'd forgotten all about them, Red! And, say—will those boys be peeved at having missed the fight!"

He was still grinning at the thought when he set the captured seaplane down on the bumpy water, in a cloud of spray. His expression changed, however, as the craft developed a sharp list to port, which grew steeper every second.

"Hey, Skipper!" cried Red Pennington, in alarm. "Those bullets must have made a sieve of our left pontoon. The wing's goin' to 'catch a crab'!"

As he spoke, the left wing tip caught a wave and

went under. The whole plane shuddered, swung about and lost the remainder of its speed. Another wave slapped loudly against the listing fuselage.

Don Winslow unsnapped his safety belt and faced around.

"Water'll be coming through those holes under our feet in a moment," he said tersely. "We'd better unlash our prisoner and get him out of here, quick!"

"Aye-aye, Skipper!" gulped Red, bending over the Scorpion pilot. "I made him fast on the deck here, seeing there were only two safety belts, and—great guns, Don! He's wounded! Bleeding from the head! Help me. . . ."

Whipping a seaman's knife from under his blouse, Don quickly cut the lashings which held the unconscious man. Turning, he slid open the metal door of the cabin.

"You go through, Red, and wait for me to pass him out," the young commander said. "The fellow's still breathing. Put on your life belt first, and make it snappy. This crate's going to end over in a minute!"

Red obeyed instantly. Without waiting even to fasten the life belt, he plunged through the open door into the water. There, clinging to the fuselage, he waited for the pilot's body to be passed out.

It came, suddenly heaved through the wave washed opening, *with Don's life belt lashed in place!*

Startled, Red Pennington lost his grip, and drifted free. A second glance at the white face bobbing above the cork belt made the man's identity certain. It was the pilot, all right. But why didn't Don come?

Before Red could more than shout his friend's name, the seaplane listed more sharply than ever, forcing the cabin door under water. Don Winslow was trapped inside. He could still dive down through the doorway and swim clear, Red thought, but the air in the cabin now wouldn't last for long.

"Don's hurt, or caught in there!" Red groaned, stroking back to the half-submerged fuselage. "If he weren't he'd be out by now. There's just one way to get him, and if that fails, we'll both go down together!"

Slipping out of his unfastened life belt, he dived under the plane's wave-battered fuselage, groping for the door. A moment later he found it.

The cabin was dark, half full of water, and almost upside down. It took a few seconds for Red to get his bearings. As his eyes got accustomed to the dim light, he made out the pale blur of Don Winslow's face.

The young commander was clinging weakly to a seat, his eyes closed. As Red Pennington reached him, he stirred and mumbled vaguely, but did not release his grip on the seat. A bloody gash on his temple explained his half-conscious condition.

"Must have struck his head, just before the plane turned over!" the stout lieutenant groaned. "Come on, Don, old man! Leggo that seat, and lemme take you out. Leggo, I say! This plane is sinkin' lower every minute!"

Don Winslow's fingers were locked as if in a death

grip. By main force Red pried them loose and dragged his friend down toward the submerged door.

"If only he doesn't breathe in a couple lungfuls of water!" the worried lieutenant muttered, "but I've got to take that chance."

The shock of cold water closing over his head seemed to rouse Don's fighting instincts. Halfway through the doorway, he clutched at the jamb and got a grip. Red, also under water, struggled until he thought his lungs would burst.

Just in time, Don's muscles relaxed. With his last strength Red Pennington dragged him free and up to the surface. Then, all at once, strong hands were hauling the two half-drowned officers into a boat.

The next thing Don Winslow knew, he was back in his own berth aboard the *Gatoon,* with Michael Splendor, Red, and the ship's doctor crowding the little stateroom. His head still ached from the wallop he'd got inside the plane's cabin, but the bandage which the doctor had just applied felt cool and comfortable.

"Say, Doc," he grinned, trying to sit up, "who was it that beaned me this time?"

XIV

THE MYSTERIOUS CAPTIVE

It was the medical officer who actually spilled the story of Red's heroic act, in dragging Don from the sinking seaplane. The stocky lieutenant himself would never have let the real facts be known. He hated to be made a hero. As it was, he could only shake his head and scowl while the ship's doctor heaped praises upon him.

The doctor didn't leave anything out. He had been in the boat which put off to the seaplane from the *Gatoon,* and he'd seen about all there was to see.

He described how Red had thrown off his life belt and dived under the sinking plane. He told how helpless the boat's crew felt, when they got there and found neither Red nor Don.

Two of the sailors had kicked off their shoes, ready to dive in after the missing officers, when suddenly the lieutenant's red head broke surface. He was gasping for breath, and the commander was completely out when they were pulled aboard.

In the excitement, said the medical officer, the Scorpion pilot, floating unconscious in his life belt, was almost forgotten. Now, everybody aboard ship was saying that Lieutenant Pennington rated a gold medal, and . . .

"Red, you old porpoise!" broke in Don Winslow, sitting bolt upright. "Give me your flipper, and stop making faces like a seasick 'boot'! I'll get square with you some day by saying *your* life—don't worry!"

Red met his commander's handclasp with a crushing grip, his embarrassment suddenly gone. He knew that Don would never try to thank him outright, or praise him in words for an act of simple loyalty. Their friendship went too deep for that sort of thing.

"And now, Doc," said Don, "I'm going to jump into a uniform and go out on deck. I see we're under way again; and I want to talk with Captain Riggs about safeguarding the ship between here and Port-au-Prince. Probably there'll be no second attack, but it's better to be prepared."

The medical officer protested. He said Don had suffered a slight concussion, along with a scalp wound. He warned that moving about could bring on a fever. But he might as well have talked to the ship's mainmast.

Don was hurrying into his clothes even before the doctor had finished speaking. He was feeling better every minute, he declared, and he wasn't going to stay below for a mere bump on the head!

As he spoke there came a knock on the door. It was Lieutenant Darnley with a queer piece of news. The prisoner Corba had been asking urgently for Commander Winslow and he refused to say why. Lieutenant Darnley thought that if the commander were well enough . . .

"I'll be with you in two shakes, Lieutenant," Don assured the *Gatoon's* executive officer. "That lad Corba knows a lot more than he has told us yet. If he's ready to spill something interesting, I'll be glad to listen."

There were only two roomy cells in the *Gatoon's* brig. With the rescued crews of the Scorpion airplanes, they were crowded to capacity. Corba and Mink shared their cell with the pilot of the seaplane who had re-covered consciousness.

Don, standing before the cell door with Red and the other two officers, noted the pilot's makeshift head bandage.

"You'll have to tend that man's wound right away, Doctor!" the young commander said sharply. "He's an enemy, in the service of a criminal chief, but he's a human being all the same. . . . Master-at-arms! Bring that prisoner along with Corba, now!"

A moment later, both prisoners were led out, hand-cuffed. The doctor took the wounded man under guard to the sick bay while Don moved off out of ear-shot with the shifty-eyed Corba.

Red, glancing down the forecastle, caught the look of amazed interest on Don Winslow's face.

"That guy Corba must be giving him some potent dope!" he remarked in an undertone. "I'd give a lot to know what he's saying!"

"You're right, Pennington," Lieutenant Darnley agreed. "Commander Winslow isn't excited easily, I've noticed, but he's sure getting that way now. Looks as if Corba was shooting the works!"

Don Winslow's air of mystery, as he returned with Corba, did nothing to allay Red's curiosity. Even when the Scorpion agent had been returned to his cell, and Lieutenant Darnley had answered a call to the *Gatoon's* bridge, the young commander refused to answer questions.

"Come along to the sick bay," he told the red-haired lieutenant. "We'll see how sawbones is progressing with his latest patient."

When the two officers entered that portion of the *Gatoon's* sick bay which served as an operating room, the handcuffed pilot was sitting in a chair under a strong electric light. A portion of his scalp had been shaved, and the medical officer was sterilizing the raw furrow left by a glancing bullet. One of the slugs which had pierced the seaplane's cabin had nearly snuffed out the Scorpion flyer's life.

It was the first chance either Don or Red had had to examine their captive's features. Strangely enough, they were not those of a criminal. If it had not been for the man's wildly staring eyes and look of pained bewilderment, they would have been almost handsome.

There was something hauntingly familiar, too, about the man's face and build. Studying them, Red decided he had seen the fellow—or his double—somewhere, and not so long ago!

If Don Winslow had the same notion, he didn't mention it. He waited until the doctor had finished work.

Only when the armed boatswain's mate stepped forward to take the prisoner back, Don stopped him.

"Leave the patient here, and give me the key to his handcuffs!" he told the surprised guard. "I'll be responsible for him. You may return to your post outside the brig."

With a puzzled "Aye-aye, sir!" the guard departed. Don closed the door and turned to the prisoner.

"Who are you?" he asked bluntly, looking the man square in the eye.

"Andre, Count Borg," the fellow replied mechanically. "I am a licensed pilot and a native of Listonia. . . ."

"Snap out of it, man!" barked Don Winslow, stepping closer. "Do you know what you've got on your wrists? Take a good look!"

Dazedly Borg's eyes dropped to the steel handcuffs, as if seeing them for the first time. With a harsh cry he leaped to his feet, his lips drawn back in a snarl of fury.

"What does this mean?" he shouted, wrenching at the clanking chain. "You dare to handcuff me like a common criminal? What right have you to confine me?"

"Sit down!" thundered Don Winslow, forcing the man back into his chair. "You are under arrest, Count Borg, in connection with a plot to destroy the United States Navy gunboat *Gatoon*. Following the orders of your criminal chief, the Scorpion, you picked up two men in life belts—"

"But, Don!" burst in Red Pennington. "The guy knows all that. Why not get down to brass tacks and make him tell something worth while—for instance, where the Scorpion has his headquarters?"

A wild laugh from the prisoner interrupted at this point. Pounding his manacled hands against his knees, the man who called himself Count Borg rocked back and forth in hysterical mirth.

"Mad! Mad!" he choked. "We are all mad and locked up in the crazyhouse! One talks about scorpions and life belts; another raves about brass tacks! But nobody tells me how I got here, and I—I cannot remember. . . ."

With a groan the fellow raised his hands to his temples. Shifting from clear, unaccented English, he began muttering to himself in some harsh, foreign tongue.

The medical officer reached for a hypodermic needle, but Don Winslow seized his arm.

"Get him a glass of cold water, Doc," the young commander advised. "This man isn't crazy. He just thinks he's nuts, because . . ."

Pulling the doctor over to the sink, Don whispered rapidly in the other's ear. Their conference lasted two or three minutes, long enough to get the goat of Lieutenant Red Pennington, who was about fed up on being a mystified onlooker.

When the doctor returned with the water, his manner was briskly professional.

"Tell me, Count Borg," he said, "just what is the

last thing you remember doing, before you woke up in the brig half an hour ago? If there has been some mistake in your identity your answer will clear the matter up."

The wild look on the prisoner's face was now gone. In its place was a puzzled frown, and his whole manner had quieted.

"There certainly *has* been a mistake, gentlemen," he replied. "But to answer your question—the last thing I recall is walking up Cherry Street toward Brooklyn Bridge, about half past one last night. I remember hearing stealthy footsteps behind me, coming closer. After that, everything is a blank!"

There was a queer silence following Borg's words. Finally, the medical officer broke it after meeting Don's glance.

"And what," he asked in a strained voice, "would you say the date was yesterday? I mean, the day of the month and the year?"

"Why—er," responded the prisoner slowly, "April fourteenth, nineteen thirty-three. Am I right?"

"Wrong, by seven years, my friend!" Don returned, stooping to unlock the handcuffs. "Your memory has done another blackout, Count Borg! The first one was when a thug knocked you out on Cherry Street, New York, in nineteen thirty-three. The last one happened this morning when you were wounded in the head by a machine gun bullet. Since you've evidently forgotten your whole life between those dates, there's no reason for treating you now as a dangerous criminal."

XV

RED GETS A SHOCK

"Listen, Skipper!" pleaded Lieutenant Pennington, seizing Don Winslow's arm. "Maybe this guy, Count Borg, isn't nuts; but *I'm* gonna be if you keep on doin' and sayin' things that don't make sense! First you get an earful of hot dope from Corba, and start actin' mysterious. Then you get chummy with a dangerous enemy agent. He raves and hollers like a maniac; so you decide he isn't crazy but only thinks he is. Now you unlock his handcuffs, and tell him what happened to him back in nineteen thirty-three just as if you'd seen it. Have a heart, Skipper! My anchor's draggin' and I'm goin' aground fast. If you won't tell me . . ."

"Belay, sailor!" laughed Don. "You'll get the whole yarn in due time. Right now, suppose you go hunt up Michael Splendor and Captain Riggs. Say I'll meet you all in the captain's quarters about fifteen minutes from now to talk over something of the highest importance. Tell Mercedes to come along, too."

Nodding glumly, Red Pennington moved to the door.

"I'll tell 'em," he replied. "But you'd better break it to them a lot easier than you've done to me. I'm driftin' onto an uncharted coast, and my compass has gone sour on me!"

The moment Red had gone, Don Winslow turned to Count Borg.

"There's no time now to explain everything, Count," he said tersely. "You must simply take my word for the moment, and believe that we mean to help you out of your present strange predicament. The facts are briefly these:

"In the past seven years you have been associated with a criminal organization which threatens the peace of many countries. This morning, you were piloting a plane which was captured with two others, during an attempt to destroy a United States Navy gunboat. You are now aboard that same gunboat under arrest for conspiracy."

"But I remember nothing of that!" protested Count Borg, with a look of keen distress. "If what you say is true, I must have lost my reason, as well as my memory, during those years which are now a blank. I am not naturally a criminal. You must believe that, Commander—er—"

"Winslow," nodded Don. "I am inclined to believe you, Count, and to test your good faith, I shall ask you to help, so far as you can, in tracking down your former criminal associates. Are you willing to co-operate with the Navy in this fight before your case comes to trial?"

"Of course, Commander Winslow!" exclaimed Borg, rising to grasp Don's hand. "I'll be grateful for any chance to undo the damage of those criminal years, when I was not myself! But, tell me, what on earth can I do to help, without a memory?"

"First," answered Don Winslow with an enigmatic smile, "you can shave off your moustache!"

In the meantime a curious and impatient group awaited Don Winslow's appearance in Captain Riggs' cabin. To while away the minutes, Mercedes and Red discussed the recent air battle, and the disappointment of the Navy fliers in arriving too late for the scrap.

"They did accomplish one thing, though," put in Captain Riggs. "That big bomber they call a flying fortress brought us a couple of new parts for our anti-aircraft guns. The gunner and his mates are mounting them now, so we'll not be helpless against another attack between here and Port-au-Prince. Not that the Scorpion is likely to strike again so soon!"

"I quite agree with ye, Captain!" said Michael Splendor. "We'll be in port by nightfall, and from there 'tis but a short run by motorcar to my villa in the hills. Our friends can rest safely there and enjoy themselves, until orders come from Washington. . . . By the way, did you say the pilot of that seaplane was called Count Borg?"

"That's what the guy called himself, Mr. Splendor," replied Red, disgustedly. "Don seemed to believe him, but I'd think twice before takin' the word of a nut like that. He sure was raving!"

"Was he, now?" murmured the cripple with a sly wink. "Indeed, Lieutenant, I should say a man with a bullet dent in his skull might be excused for a bit of ravin'. However, if the man is Count Borg, I can tell you something about him. He is one of the aces in Scorpia's evil organization—a man of great resource and daring and very useful to his chief. I have never seen him, personally, but while I was a captive of Cho-San and his fiendish master, I heard Borg's name mentioned frequently."

"If he's one of their 'key' men," put in Mercedes, "his capture is going to put a crimp into the Scorpion's style, isn't it, Mr. Splendor?"

"We've already put quite a crimp into the Scorpion's style, bad 'cess to him!" snorted the man in the wheel chair. "In the last thirty-six hours, we have seized some of his most valuable inventions, blown up his submarine base, arrested three of his agents aboard this ship, foiled his plans to destroy the *Gatoon,* shot down three of his fast bombing planes, and captured five members of their crews alive. That does not mean, however, that we have crippled his power for evil! Men and machines can be replaced, for Scorpia's wealth is immense. No, me friends! We have struck no vital blow as yet; but I'm thinkin', perhaps, through this Count Borg . . . Ah, Commander! I was wonderin' when ye would join us and tell us what ye've found out."

Turning about, he motioned the newcomer to the empty chair beside that of Captain Riggs. Red Pennington got up and closed the skylight. Mercedes moved to the other end of the cabin locker beside Michael Splendor.

"You're pale, Don!" the girl said anxiously, as the tall young officer took his seat. "Are you sure you feel able to be up, with your wounded head? And your eyes are *queer!* As if you were looking at me for the first time in your life!"

"I am!"

The voice which spoke those two words was Don's; yet there was a strange note in it, which shocked everyone in the cabin to attention.

"You see," it continued hollowly, "I am not Don Winslow!"

"OH!"

Mercedes' shriek cut the horrified silence like a knife. All at once she was beside the young man, gazing fixedly into his eyes, as if to read the brain behind them. While the others watched her, fascinated, she stepped slowly back.

"No! No!" she sobbed, covering her face with her hands. "You are not Don. Oh! What right have you . . ."

"Skipper!" pleaded Red Pennington, laying a hand on his friend's shoulder. "Come on back to your berth! I was afraid that would get you feverish . . . Captain Riggs, help me take him—"

"WAIT, GENTLEMEN!" cried the young officer rising suddenly to his feet. "I am sorry to distress you, but I have been simply obeying orders. Commander Winslow is standing there in the doorway!"

Instinctively all eyes followed his pointing finger, only to stare in stark unbelief.

There *could not* be two Don Winslows. Yet there in the doorway stood the young officer's double, complete in every detail. Even the paleness and the white bandage about the temple were reproduced in each figure.

"It's a trick!" cried Captain Riggs hoarsely. "The Scorpion has hypnotized us—or tried to! But there's one way to break any spell!"

Tugging a blunt nosed pistol from his pocket, the *Gatoon's* master would have fired at the man in the doorway, had not Michael Splendor driven his wheel chair between them.

"Stop it, Riggs!" bellowed the gray-haired cripple. "If ye value your own life, not to mention Commander Winslow's, lower that weapon, sir! Miss Colby is right! The gentleman at the table is a stranger; but the man here beside me is Don Winslow himself, may heaven preserve him!"

Impulsively, both Mercedes and Red had to feel of the real Don's hands and features to make sure he was not a dream figure, as Riggs still seemed to think. After that, Red stepped across to the man by the table.

"I know you now, mister!" he grinned sheepishly. "You're the one the doctor was working on in the sick bay. The man who said he was a count! You had a moustache on then."

"Count Borg is my real title, Lieutenant," smiled the other. "Commander Winslow wished me to impersonate him, in order to test out our strange likeness. It seems that even our voices are much the same in pitch and timbre. You see, if I can impersonate *him* so successfully as to fool his closest friends, he should be able just as easily to trick those who know *me*!"

XVI

DANGER AND A WOMAN

"It was Corba who put me wise to that resemblance," Don told the astonished group after Borg had left. "That radioman is a born traitor, and he's figuring every possible way to cross up his old pals in hope of getting in right with us. He suggested that I might use my likeness to Count Borg as a means of spying on Scorpia's activities. It certainly looks like a hot idea; but I'd want your opinion of it, Mr. Splendor, before going farther with any plans."

"It will take a bit of study, I can see that," replied the veteran Intelligence man. "But first of all, Commander, why ye think Count Borg is not planning a clever trap for ye? He's too bright a man to be a common double-crosser like Corba. Mind ye, he has been one of the Scorpion's most trusted agents. Considerin' that, it strikes me he fell in with your impersonation scheme a bit too quickly. It's not like him to play traitor to his chief."

"Which is the very reason I believe he will be loyal to our cause now!" retorted Don, his eyes narrowing thoughtfully. "You see, Mr. Splendor, our man has been a victim of *amnesia*. The bullet wound he received this morning restored his memory of everything that happened until the night of April fourteenth, nineteen thirty-three. At that time his skull was fractured by a thug's blackjack. Of the seven years between then and now he has not the slightest recollection."

"Amazin', if true!" muttered the cripple, meeting Don's level look. "Are ye sure, Commander, that this *is* amnesia, and not another clever piece of actin'? Count Borg is no ordinary man, remember. He'd be quite capable of plannin' a trick like that from the moment he found himself aboard ship!"

"He couldn't fake amnesia well enough to fool an expert," Don pointed out. "Our medical officer happens to have made a special study of brain disorders, and he says this is a genuine case. Doc thinks that Borg's first injury changed his whole character. Recalling little except his name, the man became an obedient tool of Scorpia. He remembered no other friends, no other life; and his naturally keen brain was completely at the service of his criminal master. Now, of course, he is horrified at the idea of having been one of that crowd. He wants to make up in some way for the damage he has done as a Scorpion agent."

"But what luck it would be, Don," put in Mercedes, "if Count Borg *should* start to remember his life as one of Scorpia's aces! He might give us enough information to clean up the entire organization in one swoop. Of course that sort of luck is too good to be real!"

"I'm afraid it is, my dear," said Splendor. "However, I think we have a chance of getting most, if not all, of the evidence we need, thanks to this resemblance between Don Winslow and his captive. Do ye recall the code message we discovered at the submarine base— the one which Corba later stole from your stateroom, Commander? Well, I had the master-at-arms search all five of our new prisoners before ye were on deck this mornin'. And every last one of them had the same code message tucked away in his clothing! Ye see what that means?"

"Hmmm! It looks as if the Scorpion were calling all his forces together at San Francisco for some big job, if you ask me," Don answered soberly. "That would be the very thing to get in on—a general conference of Scorpia's operatives. If I got out of it alive, we'd have enough evidence to hamstring the organization's power for years to come!"

"That's all very well, gentlemen," growled Captain Riggs, picking up his hat, "but I believe you're going to find some pretty big difficulties in the way. Unless Borg recovers his memory and gives you the Scorpia passwords, not to mention a lot of other information, I fear your disguise won't get you very far, Commander. You'll excuse me if I leave you now to take my watch on deck!"

With a brusque nod the *Gatoon's* master closed the cabin door behind him. Mercedes looked across at Don, her eyes dark with anxiety.

"I'm afraid Captain Riggs is right about that," she said. "Oh, Don, I hope you'll not attempt anything so risky as to pass yourself off for the count! There are a thousand details on which your ignorance would trip you!"

"There's a way out of that difficulty, Skipper," spoke up Red Pennington. "Suppose we give out a story that Borg has escaped. Actually of course, he'll stay in plain sight dressed in your uniform. You'll be the one who disappears and shows up in San Francisco as Count Borg. You'll pretend that your memory is partly blacked out by your head wound and that will account for any slips you make, like forgetting people and passwords that Borg used to know."

"Great stuff, sailor!" cried Don Winslow, leaping up to pound Red enthusiastically on the back. "That story will have enough truth in it to convince the most suspicious Scorpion operatives. What do you think of it, Mr. Splendor?"

The man in the wheel chair wagged his gray head.

" 'Tis a clever plan—very clever indeed," he admitted. "As a matter of fact, I can think of only one person in Scorpia's ranks whom it would not fool. When I was stationed in San Francisco it was reported that a certain beautiful young girl was in love with Count Borg . . ."

"A woman!" cried Mercedes Colby. "That tears it, Don! Remember, I was the only one of us who knew that Count Borg was not you? A woman's instinct will tell her the truth, in spite of the most perfect disguise. If you meet this girl, as you surely will, she'll know you're not her lover. By the way, what is her name, Mr. Splendor?"

"They call her the Lotus," chuckled the gray-haired cripple. "Some say that she is part Chinese, others that she is of pure white blood, brought up by Chinese who kidnapped her in infancy. All agree that she is very lovely and *very* clever having been trained by Cho-San himself."

"Then she is all the more dangerous!" Mercedes protested. "Please, Don! Give up this wild notion of putting yourself into Scorpia's power, for that is just what you would be doing! You might be able to disguise your identity from men, but never from a woman in love!"

"Maybe," suggested Red Pennington, "this gal Lotus isn't in love with Count Borg any more. A lot of things have happened since you were stationed in 'Frisco, Mr. Splendor. And a dame like that *could* change her mind, you know."

"Sure, 'tis entirely possible, Lieutenant," the older man agreed. "I'll think over the whole proposition between now and the time we drop anchor in Port-au-Prince. On the way to my villa in the mountains we can talk again, me friends. Will that suit you?"

"It ought to, Mr. Splendor!" smiled Mercedes rising from her chair. "In the meantime, Don and Red are going to rest undisturbed, if I have to stand guard at the door. After swimming all night and fighting all morning, they've got to get some sleep!"

With sleepy grins, the two young officers steered obediently for their stateroom. Tumbling into their berths, clothes and all, they knew nothing more until the cabin steward called them for mess that evening.

The ship had already dropped anchor in the harbor of Port-au-Prince, and Don and his friends were eager to go ashore at the first possible moment. After a hastily eaten meal, they shook hands with the *Gatoon's* officers, and stepped into the gunboat's launch.

At the dock Splendor's pilot, Panama, met them with a powerful car. For ten minutes they dodged and twisted through the city's quaint old streets, then struck into a fine, smooth road leading toward the hills.

"Ah, me friends," sighed Michael Splendor, as the big twelve cylinder car picked up speed, " 'tis great to be gettin' home again after, the last few days of excitement! I'm well along in years now, and risks are not so thrilling as they used to be. I'd rather be sittin' by me own fireplace in peace and comfort."

Panama's amused chuckle drifted back from the front seat.

"You didn't act that way, sir, when you were slamming bullets into those two Scorpion bombers!" he observed. "And when some of their slugs ripped into us, it just made you all the happier—to judge by what I heard!"

"Whisht, lad!" growled the veteran, scowling ferociously. " 'Twas naught but the Irish blood of me enjoyin' the scrap. A true son of Erin always howls when he fights; but me brain was tellin' me all the while that war is a horrible business, even when you're fightin' to stop it. And that reminds me, Commander! I've made certain arrangements to further your scheme for impersonatin' Count Borg!"

XVII

ORDERS FROM WASHINGTON

"You mean," asked Mercedes, as the little party sat sipping their after dinner coffee on Splendor's wide veranda, "that you actually approve of Don's risky plan? To me it seems like taking a hundred-to-one chance. There are so many traps he might walk into whichever way he turns!"

"Aye, there's no denyin' the dangers," Michael Splendor agreed solemnly. "But there are ways of lessening them, I think. Take that treacherous radioman, for instance, he is only too anxious to talk, and he knows a great deal that will be useful to Don Winslow. The other captives have not been persuaded to loosen up."

"Then you've interviewed them all?" queried Red Pennington, in surprise. "Gee, you must have been busy while Don and I were pounding our ears this afternoon! But how're we gonna get hold of Corba again? I heard Captain Riggs sayin' that he was shovin' off again in the morning."

"And so he is," said Splendor. "But tonight, some time durin' the wee, small hours, another closed car will be comin' out here from Port-au-Prince. Inside of it will be Corba and our new friend, Count Borg, under guard, of course. We'll have a talk with them tomorrow, providin' Headquarters okays Commander Winslow's scheme. We should be hearin' any minute from the phone call I put through to Washington."

As he spoke, there came the faint ringing of a telephone bell, somewhere in the villa's spacious interior. A moment later a soft-footed native servant approached Michael Splendor's chair.

"*C'est pour, M'sieu'* Don Winslow!" the man murmured in soft Haitian speech.

"There's your call, Commander!" the young officer's host interpreted. "I put it through to Captain Holding in your name. Tell him the whole scheme as ye worked it out, and add that I'm helpin' ye with the details. Here's hopin' ye persuade him!"

With a sober nod Don followed the servant through the wide doorway into the house. When he had gone, Mercedes turned to Splendor with a troubled frown.

"How do you know," she said, "that this telephone conversation won't be overheard? There is such a thing as wire tapping, you know. And couldn't a radiophone message be intercepted by anyone who turned in to the right wave length? If the Scorpion's agents should get wind of Don's plan, it would be worse than useless to go ahead!"

"Your reasoning is excellent, my dear," the man in the wheel chair answered. "I believe, however, that the chance of our friend's words being overheard is less than if he and Captain Holding were sitting in the same room. Commander Winslow is sitting this minute in a soundproofed booth. The wire is connected with me own private radio room, where it is hooked up with a powerful radio beam transmitter. If an airplane with its radio tuned just right should blunder into that beam between here and Washington, the pilot might do a bit of eavesdroppin'. But the chance is one in a billion, I fancy!"

Reassured, Mercedes sank back in her chair.

"I guess it's foolish for me to worry about such things," she admitted. "You seem to have thought of every detail in advance, Mr. Splendor. I don't see any armed guards patrolling about, but I suppose we're safer here in your wild Haitian hills than we were on the high seas, aboard the *Gatoon!*"

Enthusiastically Red Pennington took up the same theme. He had seen enough of Michael Splendor's shrewd planning to believe the veteran capable of handling any situation, on land or sea or in the air.

That private beam radio was the last word in preparedness, the chubby lieutenant stated. As for guards about the premises, what good would they be, he asked, if they simply strutted back and forth in plain sight like any cop on a beat?

Starting from there, he became really talkative. He praised his host's magnificent grounds and living quarters, and especially his kitchen staff. In the meal they had just eaten all Red's dreams of earthly happiness had come true, he declared. With a cook like that, he didn't see how Michael Splendor could bear to miss a single meal at home!

"Sure, I've other duties than stuffin' me face, Lieutenant!" retorted the older man with a laugh. "I admit that I do meself well, though, back here in the hills, and 'tis a grand place to rest up after a long trip. I hope ye and the Commander and Admiral Colby's daughter will enjoy your stay with me; be it long or short!"

"I'm afraid," spoke Don Winslow from the doorway, "that it's going to be short, so far as I am concerned, Mr. Splendor! I've just finished talking with Captain Holding at the Navy Intelligence Office. He's ordered me to leave at once, by plane, for San Francisco!"

"You—you mean, Don, he's approved your taking the place of Count Borg?" gasped Mercedes, starting up from her chair.

"Sure, Skipper, I knew he'd do that!" Red Pennington chimed in. "But what did he say about me? If you're bound for 'Frisco, I'm going right along with you, y'know. You can't scuttle a shipmate in mid-voyage!"

There followed a lively argument, with Red and Mercedes trying to beat down the protests of Don and the crippled Intelligence chief. The latter pointed out, quite logically, that two disguises would be more than twice as dangerous as one. Besides there was no real need, they said, for Red to risk his life as a bodyguard for the pretended Count Borg. If Don *should* be discovered in that disguise, a whole platoon of fighting men couldn't save his life.

In the end, however, Red won his point. It was agreed that he should accompany the pseudo Count as his valet, at least as far as the Empire Hotel in San Francisco. After they registered there, of course, anything might happen.

At present, the main task for all four friends lay in getting the two young officers started on their long flight to the West coast. Captain Holding had urged haste, yet there were many things to be done.

Among these was the job of pumping the Scorpion radioman, Corba, for every scrap of information about the real Count Borg. Michael Splendor volunteered to do the pumping, so that Don and Red might rest up for the hard trip ahead.

Meanwhile, it was decided Panama would be overhauling Splendor's big, new cabin plane for a nonstop flight. The following night it would be ready, in its hangar behind the villa, for the supposed Count Borg to "steal." When that was done and the "escaping prisoner" was well on his way, the alarm would be spread. No mention, of course, would be made of Lieutenant Red Pennington's disappearance at the very same time!

With Don and Red taking turns at the cabin plane's controls, they should arrive at San Francisco fresh enough for whatever adventures lay in store for them. The plane would be abandoned outside the city. An hour or two later, "Count Borg" would register at the Empire Hotel, with his valet, "Penny," and the dangerous game would begin.

XVIII

THE DARK FIELD

Two evenings later a heavy fog blanketed the San Francisco waterfront, hiding its smelly wharves and damp alleys under a dreary pall. A distant foghorn sounded dismally above the lap-lap of harbor water against wooden piles. Vaguely the blended roar of a mighty city drifted seaward through the murk and mist. It was a night for secrecy; for furtive business which could not bear the light of day.

In the winding alleys of old Chinatown brooded a heavy silence, spiced with queer oriental odors. It flowed between the buildings like a deep, mysterious river. It reached thick tentacles up a steeply sloping street to close around a huge stone house.

A high stone wall, clamy with the fog, surrounded the lightless edifice. Within there seemed to be neither sound nor life nor movement. Yet a sharp-eyed passerby might have noticed a tiny thread of light peeping through the drawn curtain of a second floor window.

At least the light was there, although blurred and scarcely visible in the close-pressing fog.

One thing no curious passerby could have guessed— the luxurious richness of the room behind that drawn curtain. Soft shaded lights spread their glow over satin wall hangings, deep piled oriental rugs, and beautiful costly furniture. The air was heavy with incense, sweet but oppressive.

At a table a young woman sat gazing at her reflection in a large mirror. Clad in a loose, flowing gown of silk, her figure was almost girlish. Her face beneath its oriental coiffure had a fresh, flowerlike beauty which deepened as she turned and spoke.

"Suzette!" she murmured plaintively. "Do you think I am as lovely tonight as I was three months ago?"

A trimly uniformed maid appeared from an alcove beyond the dressing table. Her bright eyes took in the dark-haired girl in one swift, approving glance.

"But yes, Mademoiselle! You are even more beautiful tonight!" she answered. "It is that little touch of *tristesse* which make you so, I think. Is it because you are impatient to see Count Borg again after three long months? Ah, Madomoiselle Lotus! You cannot fool the little French maid, Suzette!"

With a laugh, the girl called Lotus shrugged her pretty shoulders.

"After all, Suzette," she retorted, "the Count is much more charming than the desperadoes, white and yellow, which surround us here . . ."

"Sh-h-h! Please, Mademoiselle!" the maid whispered sharply. "Please do not talk that way in this house. It is not safe! To be sure, we *think* the others have all gone out for the night, but all the same, there are things even Mademoiselle must not say!"

"Oh, bother!" cried the younger woman, springing

up with small fists clenched in anger. "I know what you mean, Suzette! And I am tired of measuring all my words to suit the great Cho-San. I am sick of looking out for eavesdroppers and spies—yes, *spies*—who run to him with reports of all I say or do! Let me tell you this, my little maid, if I ever find *you* have been bearing tales about me, it will not be well for you!"

Stamping her slippered foot, Lotus turned to the window and savagely flung up the lower sash. Through the parted curtains she leaned out, drawing in deep breaths of the foggy night air.

"But, Mademoiselle!" cried the little French maid in a tone of keen distress. "Suzette have nevair bear the tales to anyone. You do her a wrong to think she would —w'at you call—double cross Mademoiselle. She only warn you that Cho-San, he is jealous w'en you speak of Count Borg!"

"Jealous, is he?" spat the girl, whipping around to face her maid. "But I don't love Cho-San! I—I think I am too young to be in love with anybody. I like Count Borg, because he is young and handsome, and—well, he's *different*. Cho-San is a great man. He is older and stronger and he has the ear of the Master. But sometimes Cho-San forgets that he and Lotus are not of the same race!"

Gently, yet with determination, Suzette took her mistress' hand and led her back to the chair.

"Mademoiselle excites herself too much!" she murmured, picking up a brush and running it through the girl's shiny, dark hair. "Suzette, she know w'at is the reason. You are wonder if Count André Borg have make good his escape from Haiti. Evair since Monsieur Michael Splendor broadcast the stealing of his big cabin plane, the friends of Count Borg have wonder if he will dare to fly straight here."

"He'll try, anyway, Suzette," cried the girl. "He knows that Cho-San has called a general meeting for day after tomorrow night. André will be there unless something terrible happens to him between here and Haiti. Oh, it seems like years since I saw him last!"

"And now it may be only hours till you see him again," murmured the little maid. "Oh, I know how you feel, Mademoiselle! But now we must hurry, so you will not be late at the appointment downtown which Cho-San has made for you tonight. I heard him tell you it was important."

While Lotus was worrying over the whereabouts of Count Borg, the Count's double was speeding through the night sky less than a hundred miles east of San Francisco.

Already Don Winslow was training himself mentally for the part he was to play. In talking with Red Pennington who occupied the co-pilot's place in the big cabin plane, he tried to imitate the very tone and accent of Count Borg's speech.

Red, on the other hand, was training himself for the part of Penny, the Count's valet-to-be. Only for brief periods during the trip had he dropped the pose of a manservant, for he knew that his part must be played to perfection from the moment they met the first Scorpion agent.

"Do you know the place we are supposed to land, sir?" he queried in his most respectful tone. "Even if one is acquainted with the city's outskirts, it won't be easy to find an unlighted field at night."

"That will all be taken care of, Penny," replied the pseudo Count Borg. "According to the last code message we got from Haiti at least one man will be there to meet us with a fast car. Undoubtedly he will light a couple of ground flares as soon as he hears our motor overhead. Anyhow, judging by the highway lights ahead, we're almost over the spot which Splendor described."

"But supposing, sir," objected "Penny," "that one of the Scorpion stations picked up Mr. Splendor's broadcast and was able to decode it! In that case perhaps the man who is waiting for us will be a Scorpion agent backed by an armed gang. If they *should* suspect anything wrong they wouldn't hesitate to rub us out and ask questions later—not that gang!"

The idea was startling enough as "Penny" expressed it. But "Count Borg" showed no trace of nervousness.

"Of course anything is possible with that gang, as you call them," he agreed; "but Navy secret codes aren't easily broken down, even by experts. Besides I've got a feeling our number isn't up yet—look, Red! There are the ground flares being lighted now! Over to starboard, and about two miles north. We'll come down just between them, and upwind!"

The rough field lighted by the flares turned out to be a sandy patch between two highways and far from any lighted house. This much Don Winslow guessed as he set his wheels down with a gentle bump. When he had braked to a stop beyond the flares, both of them were suddenly blacked out, leaving earth and sky pitch dark.

"That's so no chance-passing motor cop will see lights and start to investigate, I guess," remarked Red Pennington, sliding back the plane's sliding door. "We wouldn't want our arrival noted on the San Francisco Police Blotter, would we, Don?"

"Hardly!" smiled the young commander, switching off the cabin light. "Out with you, now, shipmate! There's a car headed this way across the field. Keep your hand on your automatic until we know who it is. If it should be a Scorpion reception party, we won't go down without a battle!"

The lightless car skidded to a dusty standstill ten feet from the plane. Then only its head lamps flashed on, and into their blinding radiance stepped a well-built man in civilian clothes. Keeping both hands in sight, he faced the darkened plane and spoke.

"Commander Winslow, you and the Lieutenant may trust me without risk," he said quietly. "I am Hammond, from the San Francisco Office, and here are my identification papers. This car is at your service along with anything else you wish to ask for."

As Red was about to step out of the shadows, Don elbowed him back. It was still possible that a Scorpion machine gun was trained over the car's rear door, ready to fire at the sound of his voice.

He must make sure, without showing himself. Shielding his mouth with a cupped hand, he threw his voice along the plane's fuselage.

"Never mind the papers, Hammond," he responded. "A few words will do to show you have been in communication with our friends."

The car's spotlight showed Hammond's smile.

"Wise precaution, sir!" he approved. "How's this for a set of passwords:—Captain Holding—beam radiophone—Count Borg—Haiti—'Penny'—Michael Splendor? Or do you want more?"

XIX

A LUCKY ENCOUNTER

Pocketing his pistol, Don Winslow moved out into the glow of the car's lights.

"Thanks, Hammond!" he said simply, gripping the other's hand. "Your coming for us is going to simplify a lot of things. Come on, Red—I mean, Penny! Michael Splendor's last message told us to leave the plane right here."

As the car cut back into the highway leading to the city, Hammond leaned forward to speak to the driver.

"Drive slowly when you get inside the city's limits, Martin," he said. "Swing around past Cho-San's place before you pull up at the office."

Leaning back against the cushions, he addressed the two young Intelligence officers.

"We got the whole story by beam radiophone," he explained. "That's how we were able not only to meet you gentlemen, but also to make certain other preparations as well; such as an electric needle for giving you a scar, like the little one Count Borg has just below his cheek bone. You can only see that mark by a bright light, but it's one of the things his Scorpia friends are going to look for."

"I know about that, Hammond," Don Winslow answered. "Borg himself called my attention to it yesterday. There's the matter of his clothes, too. Borg has always been a slick dresser, and he is supposed to have escaped with a wad of Splendor's cash. That means his Scorpia pals will expect him to show up dressed like a fashion plate."

"They will," nodded Hammond. "Splendor broadcast the story of 'Count Borg's' escape with his plane and his dough. There's no doubt the Scorpion and his agents know about that. They'll expect you to show up at the meeting two nights from now, if not sooner. They'll find out about the plane having landed. Splendor's flying here tomorrow with Miss Colby on Captain Holding's orders. He'll pretend he's just trailing his stolen plane . . ."

"Z-ZZZ-ZZZZ! PR-R-R-RRH!"

A sudden loud snore from Red Pennington drowned out Hammond's voice. The chunky lieutenant had done his full share of the piloting since leaving Haiti, and was letting weary Nature have her way now.

"We'll let him sleep," chuckled Don, "until we get to your office, Hammond. We can discuss everything then."

Red's slumber, however, was due to be rudely interrupted. After skirting the edges of San Francisco's old Chinatown, the car turned up a steep hill at the top of which stood the great stone-walled house of Cho-San.

"I wanted to show you this place just in passing, Commander," Hammond was saying. "Cho-San lives here like an Oriental prince, yet his only visible income is from his curio shop down the hill. We know he's a big shot in the criminal organization of Scorpia, but we can't pin it on him. That job will be up to you, if you live to finish it! Cho-San's thugs will stop at nothing—"

BANG!

At the loud report, the car lurched sidewise, swayed another twenty yards, and stopped. Red Pennington awoke with a yell. Guns out, the three men in the back seat peered through the bulletproof windows.

They were just opposite the dark stone edifice, which was the only building within a hundred yards. Could a single shot from behind those misty walls have ripped through one of the rear tires?

It was Don Winslow who answered the question in all their minds.

"Just an accidental blowout, I think," he stated, putting away his automatic. "There's not enough light to fire a shot with any accuracy."

"You're right, sir!" muttered Hammond, following Don through the door. "I guess I'm jittery just because it happened right across from Cho-San's stone fort. Probably just an accident—"

"Is that the fort you mean?" gulped Red, with one foot still on the running board. "Gee! If they've got machine guns trained on us, isn't it kinda foolish to stick around?"

"I didn't mean a fort in that sense, Lieutenant!" said Hammond. "Cho-San's rock pile here *looks* like a fort, especially in the dark. If there's any machine guns inside, they won't be aimed at us now . . . But, say! What's that car pulling in ahead of us?"

A long, low hung, black car had boiled up the hill behind them, only to stop ten paces beyond with a squeal of gripping tires. The two young officers, with Hammond and Martin, stiffened instinctively, hands whipping to their pistols. For all they knew this might be a gang car, filled with Scorpion killers.

A door opened, and a man in uniform cap jumped out. Swiftly he moved to the rear door, opened it, and stood back waiting. From the dark interior appeared a young woman in a white evening wrap, her dark hair lighted by the flash of jewels. With a murmured word, she turned away from the car, walking quickly toward the house of Cho-San.

The four men watching her relaxed.

"That's the girl they call the Lotus!" whispered Hammond in Don Winslow's ear. "She's the one you'll have to look out for especially, Commander. Look! What's she up to, now?"

With a low cry of pain, the girl had stumbled. Now she stood swaying, as if about to fall.

"She's turned her ankle! I'm going to help her, Hammond," muttered Don. "You all stay here."

The other car, Don noted, was just driving away. Reaching the girl's side, he caught her arm firmly, taking the weight off her injured foot.

"I saw you trip," he said, imitating Count Borg's smoother tone. "What luck that I was just across the street!"

"André! André!" gasped Lotus, leaning heavily against him. "Is it really you? But yes! Your voice—your touch on my arm! I know them, though your face is queer in this light!"

"Of course, little Lotus bud!" laughed Don, slipping an arm about her shoulders. "You miss the moustache I had to shave off. But your ankle must be paining you a lot. Let me help you as far as the house!"

"To the house, André!" cried the girl. "You mean you're not coming inside? Didn't you come here to see me?"

"Please—not so loud!" warned the pseudo Count. "I can't stop longer without making the men with me suspicious. It was just the accident of a blowout that made them stop here at all. I'll explain everything when I see you next—say tomorrow night, at the Empire?"

"That's a long time to wait, André, when I haven't seen you for so long!" sighed Lotus, with a hint of disappointment. "I guess you know best, though. Suppose you meet me in the dining room, at that same little table in the corner—remember?"

"At seven o'clock," agreed Don, as the girl turned with one gloved hand on the gate latch. "And I'm awfully glad your ankle isn't really injured! Good night!"

Returning across the street, he found that Hammond's chauffeur had about finished putting on the spare wheel. Hammond beckoned both officers into the car and closed the door after him. A moment later the motor started.

"Tell us about it, Commander," the office man urged, as they turned in to a more brightly lighted section of the city. "You think the Lotus really took you for Count Borg? If she didn't, it's going to make things pretty difficult."

"I don't think you need to worry, Hammond," Don replied. "Remember, the light was very dim, so she couldn't have noticed small details. Of course, I had to explain the loss of my moustache . . . By the way, I've got a dinner date with her for tomorrow evening at the Empire!"

"That ought to give us enough time to get fixed up and coached for our parts," Red Pennington commented. "Gee, Don! What a lucky break! Our tire blowin' out, and Lotus showin' up at the same time! It all happened so naturally, not even the Scorpion himself could suspect anything queer."

"Unless," said Don thoughtfully, "the guard inside Cho-San's iron gate smelled something phony. You see, Lotus *wanted* to believe I was Borg, but that other guy may have been leery."

"A guard, huh?" snorted Hammond. "I don't like that, Commander! As you say, he just *might* have smelled a mouse. Those Scorpion agents are suspecting each other half the time, and . . . Hmmmm! You were close enough to see him plainly?"

"Only the glow of his cigarette tip," answered Don. "But why worry over that? Looks as if we'd arrived at your office already; and I'm hungry enough to eat the letters off a stone monument!"

"And those letters are sunk in, too!" laughed the Intelligence man, reaching for the door handle. "Well, Commander, there's a hot meal waiting for you right upstairs. I ordered it brought in, because you're not visiting any restaurant until your make-up is absolutely perfect."

XX

THE TEST

It was well past ten o'clock that morning before Don and Red were roused from a four-hour nap in the local Intelligence Office. After breakfast, they were fitted out with clothes quickly tailored to fit, in preparation for their new roles. Then, for several more hours they were drilled, each man in his part, so as to make the disguise as perfect as possible.

Don Winslow had already memorized all the real Count Borg could teach him. Now, working from photographs, and from a mass of information collected by the office, other Intelligence operatives expertly polished his likeness to the captured Scorpion aviator.

Poor Red was made to study much harder for his role of valet, since he had to start from scratch. At the end of six hours' unremitting work, he was pronounced a "passable fake" and sent out to take rooms for his master at the Hotel Empire.

Somewhat later Don Winslow joined him. True to the dressy habits of Count André Borg, he had to change from the natty homespun business suit he was wearing into formal "soup-and-fish."

While he was adjusting his black bow tie, there came

a rap on the door. Red Pennington, now transformed into the valet "Penny," opened it with a flourish.

"Please step inside, sir!" Don heard him say. "I believe you are expected."

"Excellent, Pennington! Excellent!" came Hammond's approving chuckle. "You're getting more stiff-necked and manservantish every minute. Shut that door, now, and let's have a few final words."

"Yes, sir! Very good, sir!" chanted Red, looking down his rather stubby nose. "But may I take your hat and coat first, sir?"

Grinning broadly, Hammond spun a chair away from the wall and sat down on it.

"The Lieutenant's eaten his part like an old actor!" he remarked. "But how about you, Commander? Do you feel able to deceive the bright eyes of the fair Scorpion spy who'll be sitting across the table from you in about ten minutes? They say a woman's instinct is foolproof. Of course, that may be all nonsense, but I've seen some queer things happen in this Intelligence game."

Don finished buttoning his vest, and let Penny adjust his Tuxedo jacket.

"No, Hammond," he smiled, "I don't feel nervous about meeting Lotus' inspection. That's queer, too, because it is probably the toughest test I'll have to pass. I've got a funny hunch about that young woman!"

"What do you mean—hunch?" growled Hammond, with a piercing look. "You haven't had time to learn anything new about her. Listen, Commander! Just because the kid is as attractive as they make 'em, you musn't go off the deep end. Keep your head, man, and remember the lovelier she looks the more dangerous she's bound to be!"

Don's hearty laugh wiped some of the worry from Hammond's gloomy face.

"I'm certainly not going to fall in love with her, if that's what you mean!" he promised. "But seriously, I *have* a hunch that if she found out who I really am, she would be sport enough to give me a break. My masquerade would be finished, but not necessarily my life. Understand?"

Hammond got up from his chair, frowning.

"I understand, but I don't agree," he said heavily. "The minute you come within speaking distance of a Scorpion spy in that disguise, your life's in danger. The second you're discovered, it'll probably be curtains whether pretty little Lotus or some squint-eyed thug puts out your light. Well, I won't be keeping you any longer. Luck, Commander! And for the luvva Mike, *watch your step!*"

Red's good-by warning was similar to Hammond's, but even more heartfelt. His right hand still half paralyzed by the husky "Penny's" grip, Don Winslow walked quickly to the hotel elevator.

Somewhat to his surprise, the operator greeted him respectfully as "Count Borg" showing that the real count was well known to the Empire staff. Don decided that he would indeed have to "watch his step"!

Lotus, he recalled, had mentioned a certain table in

a corner of the dining room, where she had met the real count on past occasions. If she should not be there waiting for him, Don would be in a fix. He could not pick the wrong table to wait for *her*, without making her suspicious.

As he hesitated just outside the dining room, the headwaiter spotted him and came forward quickly.

"Ah, Count Borg! It is good to have you with us again after so long an absence!" the man murmured with his most unctuous smile. "Is it perhaps that you are expecting Mademoiselle Lotus this evening? If so, your table in the corner is reserved for you."

With a low bow, the headwaiter led the way to a softly lighted alcove, somewhat apart from the main dining room. It held one small table suitable for two persons. The service included a single candle set in a beautifully ornamented silver candlestick.

Barely had the headwaiter pulled out Don's chair, when his alert eye caught a movement across the larger room.

"*Eh, voilà, M'sieu le Comte!*" he exclaimed delightedly. "Here is the so charming Mademoiselle already! You will not have to wait."

Hurrying away, he was back in a moment, followed by a dainty figure dressed in clinging white satin. Lotus had made herself particularly charming this evening, Don told himself. The pure simplicity of her low cut gown, made her seem even younger than her actual twenty years.

Slipping the expensive evening wrap from her shoulders, she flicked it carelessly across the headwaiter's arm.

"Come back in a few minutes, Maurice!" she said, as the man bowed himself away.

Turning to Don, she gave him a long, serious look. Her eyes, Don thought, were like great wells of darkness. As the seconds ticked past, and she did not speak, he felt a tiny shiver of doubt. Was it possible, he wondered, that the girl had already pierced his masquerade?

All at once she came closer, with a low musical laugh.

"Always mysterious, aren't you, André?" she said, taking both his hands. "Every time I meet you here, it is the same! You stand looking at me so silent and grave, until I feel like a silly little girl. But in the end I always succeed in making you laugh and be silly with me, don't I, André?"

With some difficulty Don held his serious pose. Lotus' teasing laughter and girlish sweetness were harder to resist than he had expected.

"Sit down, child!" he said soberly, as he moved to pull out her chair. "A strange thing has happened since I last saw you. You *say* I am the same André. But it is hardly the truth!"

As he sat down across the table he saw that the girl's cheeks had gone white as her dress. Her eyes, wide with sudden alarm, seemed about to overflow with tears.

"I—I don't understand you!" she whispered faintly.

For an instant, Don found it hard to go on. This child opposite him might be a Scorpion spy, even one of the cleverest, but tonight she was simply a girl in love. A very young girl, who had clearly laid her heart at the feet of her hero, Count André Borg. And Don, the pseudo André, was going to hurt her feelings cruelly.

It was a tough job, the young commander told himself, but it had to be done. In the United States Navy's war against the warmakers, sometimes the innocent had to suffer.

Bending forward, Don pushed away the sleek, dark hair just above his temple, to show the neatly taped head wound.

"That happened during the attack on the Navy gunboat, five days ago," he said grimly. "A machine gun bullet ripped through my seaplane and grooved my skull. It was Don Winslow himself who pulled me out of the water, after the plane cracked up—or so they tell me. I woke up in the brig some hours later, too dazed to know if I was afloat or ashore. Gradually my mind cleared. *But my memory has been skipping cogs ever since!*"

Slowly the look of fright left Lotus' face. Two large tears trickled down each side of her pretty nose, but her lips smiled tenderly.

"My poor André!" she cried, softly. "It must make you feel queer—as if you were someone else—to have your memory 'skip cogs'! But that is certain to cure itself! After all your brain is not like the gears of a car that have to be thrown away when they are broken. You remember *me!* Very soon you will recall everything. In the meantime, let Lotus be your memory, dear André!"

As Don Winslow gazed into her eager, pleading little face, he felt like kicking himself. Only the fact that duty came before sentiment kept him from blurting out the whole true story, then and there.

"Very well, child!" he said, glancing down at his newly manicured fingernails. "I certainly hope you are right about my mind clearing up in time; but right now I am finding this loss of memory pretty awkward. For instance, who is that large, Oriental person coming toward us? He looks as if he knew me, all right, but I can't name him, for the life of me!"

"Cho-San!" came Lotus' gasp. "Why, André! You don't even remember . . . my guardian? The greatest power in all Scorpia, next to the master? Oh, this is terrible! You must *pretend* to remember Cho-San, whatever else you've forgotten, André!"

XXI

CHO-SAN

With a cool shrug of his shoulders, the pseudo count returned to a study of his manicured fingers. He'd understood from Hammond that there was little love lost between dashing André Borg and the saturnine Chinese, Cho-San. If that were true, a pose of insulting indifference would be the safest.

In any case, it seemed to be working now. As Don continued to ignore his presence, the big Oriental stood glowering beside the table. Like a huge frog, he seemed to swell with silent rage. Suddenly he beckoned the anxiously hovering headwaiter.

"Another chair, Maurice!" he growled in a heavy bass. "Mademoiselle Lotus seems to be in the company of an idiot. I shall stay to protect her, in case he becomes a worse nuisance. Bring me a chair, quickly!"

As Maurice hurried to obey, Lotus half arose, her hands clasping and unclasping in distress.

"Please, Cho-San!" she choked. "Be patient with André—Count Borg, I mean! Five days ago he received a wound on the head, while carrying out your orders. Since then his mind has not been the same . . ."

"Evidently not!" grated the Chinese, seating himself in the chair Maurice had brought. "No man in his right mind deliberately insults Cho-San, though your André has come very near to doing so in times past. Well, Borg, have you lost your tongue as well as your reason? You had it at three o'clock this morning when you made this appointment with my ward."

"So your watchman overheard and told you about that, Cho-San!" drawled the pretended Borg, as Maurice glided away. "I thought he would, but I'm surprised you were interested enough to follow Lotus and me here. Er—by the way, it's quite true about that head wound I got. My memory has blanked out. It's only now and then I recall something that's happened in the past few years. Of course, I know you and Lotus, here; but how and why and where you came into my life I haven't the faintest idea! Awful nuisance, isn't it?"

For sixty long seconds, Cho-San stared at "Count Borg's" handsome, rather bored features. His sloe-black eyes were so wickedly penetrating that Don was glad his disguise didn't depend on paint or false hair. Even the tiny scar below his eye was genuine. For the rest, Don hoped that he had copied Count Borg's own voice and manner successfully.

At last Cho-San's big body relaxed its angry tense- ness. When he spoke, his voice had taken on a smoother inflection.

"I would give a great deal to know just *what* has changed about you, my dear Count," he remarked. "It may be your mind—in another sense of the word—for certainly you have never dared to insult me publicly before. Your alleged loss of memory is all poppy-cock, of course. It may take time to discover what your new game is, but I shall do it. Meantime, you will take my orders as before, if you know what is good for you!"

Don Winslow permitted a lazy smile to grow at the corners of his mouth.

"Oh—ah—of course, Cho-San!" he murmured, covering a yawn. "And really, it doesn't make much difference whether you believe my memory's gone or not, so long as *I* know it has. But let's stop talking about orders and insults and call Maurice back. Lotus will be much more interested in a lobster a la Newburg I am certain."

Cho-San agreed with a surly grunt, and the three orders were taken. During the meal "Count Borg" told the story he had rehearsed about his capture and subsequent escape from Haiti in Michael Splendor's plane. He made it brief but convincing, even naming the spot where he had abandoned the plane sixteen hours before.

As he talked he was aware that both the girl and her grim-faced guardian were studying him closely. What thoughts were passing through their minds, he scarcely dared to guess. Certainly Cho-San's moonlike pokerface betrayed even less than his grunted comments. Lotus, for some reason, appeared too upset for speech.

Don was glad when the uncomfortable meal was over, and Cho-San made the first motion to leave.

"I am sorry to interrupt your evening *tête-à-tête*, my dear Count Borg," the Oriental said with oily sarcasm, "but your presence is required at the comrades' headquarters. Immediately, do you understand?"

With an indifferent smile, Don moved to pick up Lotus' evening wrap.

"I told you my memory, not my understanding, had done a blackout, Cho-San," he drawled. "Lead the way, old dear, and I'll follow. Only first, I'll send upstairs for my medicine . . . Er—Maurice! Will you phone up for my valet to bring it down now with my hat and top-coat?"

"Medicine! Valet!" snarled the big Chinese, glaring furiously at Don. "What new stall is this, Borg? I tell you, I'm in no mood for trifling tonight! A man in your youth and health needing medicine—bah! And who is this manservant you've picked up? Haven't I warned you . . ."

"It's my wound, you know," cut in the pseudo count. "Ever since that bullet nicked me, I've had the most frightful headaches. Actually blind me at times! So this morning I asked a druggist chap for something, and he prescribed . . ."

"To the devil with your druggist—and with you, too, Borg!" spat the Scorpion leader. "You may think you're funny, but I do not. Lotus! Bring this fool out to the door in three minutes, or it will be the worse for you both. I'll wait for you just that long!"

Turning on his heel, the bulky Oriental stalked out of the alcove. Following slowly with Lotus, Don saw Cho-San halt and stare at the figure of "Penny" who had just appeared in the lobby. Evidently Red had made record time for a valet, after getting the head-waiter's phone call.

With a murmured excuse to Lotus, Don stepped forward to meet his manservant at a point just out of earshot.

"Listen, Red!" he whispered, taking the small bottle Pennington had brought. "I'm going for a ride with Cho-San and the Lotus in about two minutes. Follow us in another car, but watch your step. That's all for now!"

Slipping into his topcoat, he sauntered back to the girl.

"Come, little Lotus!" he said banteringly. "We musn't keep your guardian waiting. It's bad for the jolly old dragon's disposition. By the way, where are the comrades' headquarters he spoke of. I suppose I must have been there countless times, but it's all foggy in my head now."

Sudden fear showed again in the look Lotus gave him.

"I—I wonder, André," she said in a strained tone, "if Cho-San may not be partly right about the change in you. It doesn't seem possible you could have forgotten so many things! I wonder if you are not just playing a part, for some strange purpose of your own!"

There was no time for Don to think up a reply, as they were already passing through the outer door. Just across the sidewalk the huge figure of Cho-San bulked beside a waiting car.

Once inside the limousine, Don found himself in no

mood for further self-explanations. More and more it was being impressed upon him that the job he had undertaken was beset with risks. So far he had been able to dodge open failure; but this fact failed to set his mind at ease.

Cho-San, and now Lotus herself, had made it plain that they suspected something wrong with him other than a loss of memory. They seemed to take it for granted that he was really Count André Borg, yet they accused him of playing a part!

Don would have given his right hand now to know just what suspicions were seething in the minds of his two companions.

Another question popped up to startle him, as the big car rolled through San Francisco's older, dimly lighted section.

Did the real Count Borg know the Chinese language?

As if in answer to his thought, Cho-San spoke suddenly in rapid, sing-song syllables.

"Kia hing—po pay-ow ni shi lee ting!"

Don's scalp prickled as if a gun had been leveled at his head. Was this the showdown he asked himself?

"So-lay-ow!" came the chanted response from the driver's seat.

Don's lungs deflated in a sigh of relief. The Chinese syllables were not meant for him. He had the feeling of having stepped over another deadly trap.

"So Don Winslow is still in Haiti?" rumbled the Scorpion leader's next words. "Did you learn, my dear Count, anything about his further plans while you were there? For instance, does he intend to return shortly to the United States?"

"I didn't hear a thing about his intentions, Cho-San," replied Don indifferently. "I fancy, though, that he'll be in the plane Michael Splendor is flying here today. Splendor's a bit sore, you know, about my stealing his big cabin job. He broadcast the news that he was flying here on a hunch that I'd head for 'Frisco. Maybe his pilot will be this Winslow chap."

"Ummmm, I wonder!" mumbled the Oriental. "They say he looks enough like you, Borg, to be your twin. In a certain situation you might even impersonate him. Suppose, for instance, that Winslow should disappear without his friends being the wiser—just what would prevent your taking his place in the interests of Scorpia?"

Don's answer was a laugh that he tried to make natural.

"Why, my dear Cho-San," he retorted, "the interests of Scorpia would prevent my doing that to take the words out of your mouth! I admit I look like Winslow, but his voice, his walk, and everything else about him is different; so don't talk nonsense!"

"Cho-San *never* talks nonsense, you fool!" hissed the Chinese. "You will do well to remember that your life depends on your usefulness to Scorpia, and to me—its mouthpiece! If you don't, the next time a bullet strikes your skull it may be better aimed!"

XXII

WET TRACKS IN THE FOG

The big car twisted and turned through the narrow streets, boring deeper into the dark heart of old Chinatown. Don Winslow, seated between Cho-San and Lotus, felt his sense of danger rising.

At any moment now, the Chinese chauffeur would pull up at an unfamiliar building. Then, flanked by two Scorpion spies, the pretended Count Borg would enter the underworld of Scorpia.

What further tests would he have to pass Don could not guess. He knew only that if he failed his life would pay the forfeit!

Tensely he told himself that he must not fail. For the honor of the United States Navy, for the sake of his friends, and of all who prefer peace to war's mass murder, *he must not fail!*

Glancing at Cho-San, he saw that the Scorpion leader was studying a small pocket mirror, cupped in one of his huge hands. The mirror was held so as to reflect everything that could be seen through the car's rear window.

Suddenly with an angry snort, the big Chinese bent forward.

"*Yi kow pu hau-tung sai-kai!*" he cried sharply.

"Ta hau," came the driver's answering sing-song, *"kia hing."*

With a jerk the car speeded up, throwing the passengers back against the cushions. Don felt Lotus' small, cool hand close down on his finger.

"It's that car following us, André," she explained. "Cho-San has just told Ko Loo, the chauffeur, to speed up and lose it."

Don twisted to look through the rear window at the criss-crossing traffic of an intersection. With a short laugh he turned back.

"Cho-San knows best," he remarked lightly. "I couldn't tell if one of those pairs of lights back there were following us. It looks to me as if they all are. But what's the difference?"

"None, my dear Borg," rumbled Cho-San, "considering that Ko Loo has never yet failed to put an enemy off the trail. As a matter of fact, two sets of lights are following us at this moment. The trailer is being trailed by one of our own cars. He will have an unpleasant surprise, in addition to losing track of us!"

Sharp anxiety shot through Don's mind. "An unpleasant surprise" might mean anything from a car accident to murder. And Red Pennington was the trailer who was going to get it!

However, there was nothing in the world that Don could do to warn his friend. By this time both cars were out of sight. Ko Loo skidded the big limousine around two more dim corners at twenty miles an hour, and pulled up abruptly in front of a dark warehouse.

"*Ki-wo-pu teh shwoh!*" sang out Cho-San's commanding bass.

"*Ta chang!*" came the answer, as Ko Loo sprang out to obey the order. In the foggy night the chauffeur's voice had a curious, muffled sound.

Almost immediately he returned, and the car rolled silently forward into a black, cavelike opening. As it stopped, Lotus again squeezed Don's hand.

"Last time, we came another way—remember, André?" she whispered. "We are now in the garage next to Cho-San's curio shop. Of course it doesn't look like a garage from the outside with the doors closed . . ."

"*Yi ko pu hau!* I shall not need you any more, Ko Loo," interrupted Cho-San harshly. "Get out, Lotus. I'll follow you, Count Borg. Since your mind is admittedly sick, I would rather not turn my back on you, even here in my own quarters!"

"Tit for tat, and insult for insult!" smiled Don, as a brilliant light filled the room from concealed electric lamps. "You can't make me angry tonight, though, Cho-San. Not even by breaking up my evening's date with your ward! So far, your little game of hide-and-seek is most fascinating. Even as a boy, I remember . . ."

"Quite so!" hissed the Chinese furiously. "There is nothing wrong with your memory, Borg! And I can promise that you will have cause to remember *this* night if you live to be a hundred—which is not likely. Ummm-hummm! Not likely at all! Now, Lotus, if you will lead the way, please."

"Which—which way do you wish to take, Cho-San?"

asked the girl in a frightened voice. "The one through the shop?"

"Ummmm, yes. That will do," rumbled the Oriental. "It will be new, I think, to Count Borg."

"Right-o!" agreed Don airily. "I don't remember any secret passage through your shop."

"You made the last trip to the comrades' quarters by way of Cho-San's house, André," Lotus murmured, taking Don's hand. "Follow me closely now, and don't put out your hand to touch the walls!"

As she spoke a panel slid noiselessly open in the side of the room. Cho-San raised his hand to the light switch. Glancing back Don noted with surprise that the big rolling doors of the garage were now shut, though no sound had betrayed their closing.

Darkness descended like a blow as he turned his head. Don could not hear Cho-San's footsteps, though he guessed that the Chinese was moving toward him. Lotus' gentle grasp on his hand was the only thing that seemed real in that Stygian blackness. Like a blind man he followed her lead.

Meantime, several blocks away, Red Pennington perched anxiously on the seat of a skidding taxi. The driver he had picked up outside the Empire Hotel was good at this game of trailing a car on the dodge, but Ko Loo had been giving him the works.

Both the driver and his fare realized this at the same moment.

"It's this blasted fog, sir!" the former complained,

straightening out after a turn on two wheels. "I can't get close enough to see if that car ahead's the same one we're after. Not without rammin' his rear bumper! Seems to me that guy cut in from behind us while we was dodgin' cross-traffic a mile back!"

"I got the same idea, so you must be right," groaned Red, peering through the misted glass. "Look! That car's stopping—pulling over to the curb. Suppose you pull in ahead of it. I just saw something else . . ."

"Yeah? Well, all right!" grunted the driver, jamming on his brakes. "That car we just passed ain't the one we was chasin' first, so what's the diff? The meter reads ten miles an' a quarter!"

"Take that and keep the change, brother!" replied Red, shoving a bill with two figures on it into the taxi driver's hand. "I'm getting out here. Stick around for a few minutes, in case I need you!"

Not waiting for the man's thanks, he dodged across the misty street. Some two hundred feet back, the glare of the taxi's headlights had briefly picked out a gilt sign on a darkened shop front. The words Red had glimpsed were: "CHO-SAN'S *Antiques and Curios.*"

Now, whipping a small flashlight from his pocket, he read the sign again, from the distance of a few feet. The shop, whose window was curtained, seemed neither large nor pretentious. On either side were warehouses closed by high, sliding doors. The blank, uninteresting walls were in need of paint and spotted with torn bill posters.

"Some dump!" Red Pennington muttered to himself.

"Well, I had to take a look at what was under that sign, even if it didn't do me a whale of a lot of good! We lost Don's car so far back that there's no use guessing where it—Huh! THAT'S something I didn't see before!"

The flashlight beam, pointing downward, had picked out the marks of wet tire treads crossing the sidewalk at his feet. The tracks disappeared under the big rolling doors of the warehouse to the left of Cho-San's shop.

Sometime in the past hour, perhaps in the last few minutes, a car had gone in there!

As Red stood there pondering, he heard a motor start up behind him. At the moment, however, it did not seem important. The real problem was to find proof that the car which had made those wet tracks was the one he'd been trying to follow.

Bending down, he scrutinized the tread marks by the light of his small pocket torch. The sidewalk all about them was covered with tiny droplets of moisture, he noticed. But the marks themselves were barely starting to mist over.

Acting on a sudden idea, Red threw his light on one of his own footprints made on the fog-wet sidewalk a few seconds before. Already, he saw, two or three droplets had formed on the darker spot where his heel had pressed.

The conclusion was plain. A big car, with new, expensive tires had entered the warehouse doors *less than five minutes ago!*

As Red Pennington straightened up, he made his

decision. He would take the taxi back to the nearest public telephone, call Hammond at the office, report what he had found, and then stick around on watch until relieved by a trained detective. Longer watching might attract attention, considering that he had come out minus hat or topcoat.

A few quick steps took him across the street to the car which was waiting at the curb.

"Okay, brother!" he said, jerking open the rear door and ducking inside. "Back to the nearest phone booth, and make it snappy! There's another ten spot in it for you if—Say! What tha ding-dong . . . *This isn't my taxi!*"

XXIII

THE CHINESE CABINET

At the end of fifty steps in a darkness so thick that it could almost be felt, Lotus pressed Don's hand, signaling a halt. As she did so, there sounded the soft whir of hidden machinery.

"We arrive at the gateway of a secret world, my dear Count!" boomed Cho-San's bass voice from somewhere behind them.

The man's voice echoed strangely as if thrown back by the arches of the unseen tunnel. For all his effort at self-control, Don Winslow felt a shiver of apprehension creep up his spine at the eerie sound of it.

"I've never had a fancy for this underground stuff, Cho-San," he answered, forcing a laugh. "It's not in an airman's line, you know. Give me the freedom of the sky, every time, and you can have your underground ratholes!"

"Hush, André!" cried Lotus softly, clinging to his arm. "Scorpia must operate not only in the air, not only on sea and land, but *underneath* them as well. You know that as well as anybody. See, now! The panel is opening, and we step through into Cho-San's shop, where you have been many times."

As they emerged into the dimly lighted curio shop, the soft whir of machinery ended with a click.

Glancing over his shoulder, Don saw the big Chinese standing behind him against a blank wall. There was no sign of the opening through which the three of them had just passed.

"Neat, very neat indeed, Cho-San!" murmured the pseudo count. "But, tell me, which way do we go from here to the comrades' quarters? My recollection is still a bit vague, although this room does seem familiar . . ."

"The cabinet!" broke in the Scorpion leader shortly. "That way is the quickest. And I am tired of hearing about your infernal memory, Borg! Open the cabinet, Lotus!"

Obediently the girl crossed to a huge cabinet of ebony wood, and twisted one of its curiously carved dragons' heads. With scarcely a sound the door swung wide, leaving an opening the size of a full grown man. How far back the space extended Don could not see from where he stood.

"Step in, Lotus, and show your André the way!" sneered Cho-San. "You act, Count Borg, as if it were a trap. Don't worry, I am following you both inside!"

The Chinese suited his action to the word, closing the cabinet door after him. Again Don caught the smooth, scarcely audible hum of oiled machinery somewhere near by.

"More darkness!" he sighed after a number of seconds had ticked by in silence. "Really, Cho-San, a nice bright electric bulb here would cheer things up! By the way, I thought we were going somewhere in a hurry. This jolly old cabinet . . ."

"Silence, fool!" gritted the Oriental. "You are no longer in the cabinet you entered a moment ago. That ancient work of art is now standing as you saw it, far above us. Only its floor is missing, for that is now beneath our feet!"

"And here we are almost at the entrance to the comrades' quarters!" cried Lotus, as the elevator floor quivered briefly. "Now I shall press another invisible button, and you shall see that I am right, André. There will be plenty of light where we are going."

Once more a panel slid aside to show a narrow, dimly lighted corridor. This one seemed to be dug out of bedrock, with rough corners projecting. Slipping into it, the girl disappeared around a jagged corner.

"She'll get hurt dodging around those rocks!" Don exclaimed. "Where's she gone, anyway? Why didn't you stop her, Cho-San?"

"Because she is in no danger—as yet!" purred the big Chinese. "The little Lotus has been brought up in these subterranean passages and rooms. She knows her way where you, my dear count, would lose yours a hundred times over. Just now she has gone to turn up more lights so that you can see to follow."

As he spoke, the rough passage was flooded with sudden brilliance, far greater than necessary, Don thought. As he stepped away from the elevator toward Lotus' waiting figure, Cho-San himself volunteered the explanation.

"There are machine guns covering every turn on this passage, Borg," he chortled evilly. "You cannot see them, so you must take my word. Under these brilliant lights they could mow down any police forces which might be unlucky enough to come this far into Scorpia's underworld, or anyone trying to escape from it. A very comforting thought, don't you agree?"

Don's only answer was a shrug of his smoothly tailored shoulders. The next moment he was at Lotus' side picking his way over the tunnel's uneven floor.

Around the second turn the girl halted, and reaching up, inserted her fingers behind an angle of the damp stone. As if by magic a door-sized section of the rock wall moved back, disclosing a furnished apartment.

Don stepped through the opening, closely followed by Cho-San. At the soft click of a falling latch, he did not even bother to turn. The wall through which they had just passed would show no sign of a doorway, he was certain.

For the first time since leaving the car in the garage, the Chinese now seemed to drop his air of ugly suspicion. His moonlike face was almost smiling as he turned to face Don.

"I will leave you, my friend, for a short while," his deep voice intoned. "The little Lotus will remain to entertain you, so that the time will not pass too heavily. If there is anything more you may desire before I return, simply touch that bell by the table."

With a parting nod his huge figure vanished behind a tall, carved screen. Don Winslow stood gazing at it thoughtfully for a long moment, then turned to his small companion.

"Well, little Lotus," he began, "I hope your memory never starts playing tricks on you like mine. This room, for instance—"

A strange expression in the girl's dark eyes stopped him short. Following her look and gesture he stepped quickly to the inlaid teakwood table.

The thing looked innocent enough. It's decorated top bore nothing but a vase and a small lacquered tray. One glance underneath, however, explained Lotus' silent warning.

Fastened to the underside of the table top was a compact little dictaphone, no doubt being used at this moment by a Scorpion eavesdropper!

Back at the spot where he had first stood, Don picked up the conversation.

"This apartment *does* seem vaguely familiar," he continued. "It's like something I dreamed about long ago. Perhaps if you showed me the other rooms it might all come back to me. Shall we try it?"

It was the cue for which the girl had been waiting. With an eager nod she led the way toward a curtained archway.

"Why, certainly, André!" she answered. "There's no harm in looking around. These are the comrades' quarters, or at least one section of them, and of course you have been here before. Beyond this hall is a small dining room, and a sort of butler's pantry. The sleeping quarters are on another level entirely . . ."

As the heavy curtains fell back into place, Don found himself in a tiny hallway, lighted by a dim overhead lamp. He was about to proceed when the girl's quick grasp on his arm halted him in his tracks.

"We can talk now," she whispered, "but we must be brief. *I know who you are, Don Winslow!*"

The shock of those words paralyzed Don's wits for the space of five heartbeats. Backing off, he reached for the small but deadly automatic pistol concealed under his left armpit. An instant later he dropped his hands.

"I am at your mercy, it appears!" he said with a twisted smile.

The girl shook her dark head. Gliding closer she lifted her eyes to stare straight into his.

"It is Cho-San, not Lotus, whom you have cause to fear," she said. "He believes you are working against Scorpia for your own interests, but he does not know the truth. I shall not tell him, Don Winslow, provided you have done no harm to Count André Borg!"

Don thought that over carefully. He read the meaning behind her words, and knew Lotus was in love with the dashing André. Besides she must be aware that Borg's advertised escape was a mere blind. Why, then, did she not take revenge, for herself and her friends, by showing up the pseudo count without delay?

Puzzled, he put a question of his own.

"If I tell you that Count Borg is safe and well, except for a head wound like mine, how can you trust my word? A man in danger of his life is apt to say anything which will save it. How do you know I won't lie to you, Miss Lotus?"

"You will not lie, for the simple reason that I am ready to believe your word," the girl answered confidently. "That way, I put myself at *your* mercy. I trust myself to your honor, which you would rather die than betray. Is it not so, Don Winslow of the Navy?"

With a silent laugh Don threw up his hands.

"You win, Miss Lotus!" he admitted. "The truth is that Count André Borg is well and will come to no harm, in spite of any past crimes he may have committed. It is a long story, but . . ."

"Stop!" cried Lotus, fiercely gripping the young officer's jacket front. "You say he is well, yet he will not be punished! Do you mean his *mind* has been injured? That wound on his head . . . No! No! I would rather have André dead than insane! Tell me! Tell me the whole truth, or I *will* call Cho-San!"

Quickly Don gave her an outline of Count Borg's strange situation, from the moment when he came to his senses in the *Gatoon's* sick bay.

"You see, Miss Lotus," the young commander explained, "your friend is a lot saner now than he was during the seven years he served Scorpia. It is fortunate for him that he doesn't recall anything of that time. To him, April, nineteen thirty-three, seems only last week!"

The girl's eyes had filled with tears that suddenly overflowed. Her small mouth quivered like a lost child's.

"Then—then he isn't my André any more!" she sobbed softly. "He doesn't remember that he ever knew me. Now I have nothing left to live for—not even one true friend!"

XXIV

CHO-SAN'S NEWS

A drooping, discouraged little figure, Lotus stumbled back to the closed curtains. As she raised a hand to part them, Don Winslow called her back.

"You are wrong," he said huskily as the girl turned. "Count Borg needs friends right now. He needs you, Lotus! One of these days he will be released. If he has no friend to whom it matters, *he's* going to feel life and liberty aren't worth much, isn't he? Answer me that!"

Slowly Lotus' small chin lifted. Her shoulders lost their discouraged droop.

"Thank you, Don Winslow!" she whispered. "André was like that, too, saying things to give me courage when all seemed hopeless. You resemble each other in more things than voice and appearance. That is why I couldn't ever betray you to Cho-San! But come! It is dangerous to talk here longer. We must return to the living room, in case Cho-San comes looking for us."

Don realized that she was right. Without a word he followed back through the curtained archway, ready once more to play the part of Count Borg. As it turned out, they were barely in time.

Lotus had just seated herself when the little French maid, Suzette, appeared silently.

"A telephone message for Mademoiselle!" the girl announced. "Cho-San requests that you take it from the apartment of Doctor Skell."

With a warning glance at Don, Lotus rose to her feet.

"You will excuse me, André?" she asked. "It seems that our evening together is doomed to be broken up . . . Suzette! Are you not glad to see Count Borg after his three months' absence?"

The maid bobbed a quaint little foreign courtesy.

"I am ver' glad to see you again, Monsieur!" she smiled, as Lotus left the room. "Did Mademoiselle have time to show you through the new apartment beyond this one? It has been made over since you were last here."

The wink which accompanied the last statement set Don's thoughts racing. Suzette's hint was plain enough. She wanted an excuse to lead him out of the room. But why? Did she have something to say that was not meant for the hidden dictaphone?

"Made over, hmmm?" Don drawled, picking up the cue where she dropped it. "No, Mademoiselle didn't show me that. Might as well kill time while she's gone by taking a look."

Rising, he followed the little maid through the same archway where Lotus had taken him. As the heavy curtains fell back in place, he was not surprised to find Suzette at his elbow. Standing on tiptoe, the French maid whispered swiftly in his ear.

"I also," he caught the softly breathed words, "know who you are, Commander!"

The shock to Don's nerves was less, this time; but before he had time to recover, Suzette pulled his ear down once more.

"We must be brief, M'sieur," she murmured, "but I will tell you that w'ich even Mademoiselle Lotus do not know. I am operative of the French Secret Service, working to discover the Scorpion's so evil plans. I listen w'en you talk with Mademoiselle behind this curtain. Of course I have hear of the so famous Don Winslow, so I tell myself: 'Suzette, you are one lucky woman! Perhaps you can help the Commander to trap the enemy tonight!' "

In silent admiration, Don offered the plucky girl his hand. How long she had been risking her life surrounded day and night by Scorpion agents, he could only guess. Both her cleverness and her courage, he knew, must be extraordinary to get away with such a feat.

"You mean we can find a way to trap them at the big meeting tonight?" he whispered breathlessly. "That's even a bigger stunt than I'd hoped to pull off! I came here to get evidence against the big shots, but if we can deal Scorpia a crippling blow at the same time . . ."

"*Oui!* That is my thought!" cut in the French woman swiftly. "But there is not now time to tell you my plan. Instead I must warn you. Something have happen to make Cho-San suspect you are not André Borg!"

"That cuts it!" groaned Don. "I must have been pulling a whole string of boners. First Lotus, then you, and now Cho-San gets wise to me . . ."

"No! No! It is not that, M'sieur!" whispered the little maid. "You have not pull the boner, and Cho-San is not sure. You see he have just got the news that Michael Splendor and Commander Winslow have arrived by plane. The Scorpion spy who saw them at the airport say Don Winslow have a wound on the head jus' like yours. That start Cho-San wondering w'ich is the real Don Winslow and w'ich is Count André Borg."

"And so," smiled Don grimly, "Cho-San sent you in to size me up and report which of the two *you* think I am! Well, so long as he isn't sure, I stand a chance to get away with it. I'll have to be more than ever on my guard now, that's all."

"Mais oui!" Suzette said loudly, pushing aside the curtains. "And now, Monsieur, that you have seen the made over apartment, is there anything else you desire? Perhaps some music from the radio, while you await Mademoiselle Lotus?"

Before Don could reply, Cho-San himself appeared from behind the tall screen. A wave of his long fingered hand disposed of the maid. As she glided from the room, the big Chinese turned slowly to face the young Intelligence officer.

"I have news for you, Count Borg," he announced in an ominous tone. "The man who is your double in voice and features has just arrived at the airport. My agent who saw him reported that the wound on his head is identical with yours. But that is not all. It seems that even the tiny scar beneath Count Borg's cheekbone has reproduced itself on the face of Don Winslow!"

For a long moment Don's gray eyes returned the Oriental's snakelike gaze. Above all things, he told himself, he must not show nervousness. Instead, he managed an incredulous laugh.

"Now, really, Cho-San," he bantered. "You can't expect me to swallow a whopper like that! Either you're pulling my leg, or your agent had one glass too many under his belt when he looked at Winslow. The Commander wouldn't have any reason to copy my facial misfortunes, you know!"

"I do not know!" snarled Cho-San, giving way to one of his sudden rages. "I have found Commander Winslow unbelievably clever on many occasions. If I thought he could lower his stiff pride to impersonate a fool, I should suspect that *your* scars were faked!"

"And that the real Count Borg is now a traitor wearing the uniform of a United States Navy Commander?" crowed Don, sinking limply onto the nearest couch. "Oh-h-h, ha-ha-ha! I never thought to see you so confused, Cho-San! Why, supposing Winslow were—ha, ha—such an idiot as to shoot himself in the head, he couldn't fake this scar under my eye, too. You can see for yourself, Cho-San. It isn't painted!"

Lurching to his feet, Don thrust his face close to that of the glowering Chinese. The effect was everything that he desired. On the instant, Cho-San's suspicion was swept away by the sheer violence of his wrath.

"Silence, you laughing hyena!" thundered the Scorpion leader. "Perhaps if your silly face *were* painted it would sicken me less! As it is, I shall use it to serve the purposes of Scorpia, in a way suggested by Don Winslow himself. Within the next twenty-four hours that young officer will disappear. At the same time you, André Borg, will take his place and carry out certain orders. With Winslow safely in our hands, we shall proceed to spread dismay in the ranks of the Navy Intelligence!"

The harsh brutality in Cho-San's voice did more than anything to reassure Don. The Chinese had evidently made up his mind that Count Borg now stood before him, and had turned his explosive energy to another problem. From now on Don's best play was obviously to agree.

As he was about to reply, a concealed buzzer sounded loudly in the room. Cho-San turned with a muttered exclamation, and hurried out by way of the carved screen.

XXV

LOTUS' CONFESSION

Puzzled and impatient, Don Winslow paced up and down the large, luxuriously furnished room. He liked to plan his moves in advance. Instead, ever since he had met Lotus in the dining room of the Empire, he had been facing one unexpected situation after another, in bewildering succession.

Whether Suzette, the French Secret Service operative, had any definite plans he could not tell. As for Lotus, he wanted another talk with her out of range from any concealed dictaphone.

A soft *click* of a latch behind caused him to whirl. There stood the girl herself, laughing, her back against the innocent-looking panel through which she must have entered.

"Excuse me, please!" she cried, coming swiftly toward him. "But your expression was so funny—as if I had stuck a pin into you. These hidden panels and underground corridors make you nervous, don't they, Commander?"

At Don's warning, "Sh-h-h!" Lotus shook her head.

"It's all right, if we speak very low," she reassured him. "I disconnected the dictaphone at the other end.

Besides, there's no one trying to listen now. Cho-San has other fish to fry just at this moment."

"What's that?" Don asked quickly. "A moment before you came in a buzzer sounded and he acted as if it were a fire alarm!"

"It was a sort of alarm," the girl replied, seating herself in one of the deep arm chairs. "Dr. Skell got a telephone message from the garage. It seems that two of our city agents caught someone snooping about the place, and wanted to know what to do with him. Not that it matters much, but Cho-San will probably want to look him over."

It mattered a great deal to Red Pennington, however, that he had let himself be caught by such a simple trick. As he sat now in the back of a strange car, under the muzzle of a thug's pistol he understood only too well what had happened.

His captors, doubtless in the employ of Scorpia, had simply threatened or bribed his own taxi driver to clear out. The two cars looked much alike in the dark, and Red had been too unsuspecting to notice the difference, until a gun poked him in the face. As he sat there fuming at his own stupidity, the second plug-ugly came back from across the street.

"I phoned de house an' asked wot ta do wid him," the fellow reported. "De guy I talked to said ta leave him in de garage tied up, and turn off de lights."

"Okay!" grunted the second mobster. "I guess the big shots wanna give him the once-over. If he's one of them Navy Intelligence ducks they'll prob'ly bump him off, or burn him in their Chinese torture room. Anyhow, it ain't none of our business . . . Come on, you punk! Git out an' put your hands behind you!"

The last words were addressed to Red, and emphasized by a wicked jab of the pistol barrel that raised a welt along the young officer's jaw. Pretending to be frightened speechless, Red obeyed, but his brain was working at top speed to figure out a break.

At the first touch of the gangster's rope, Red's crossed wrists flew apart. Sweeping up, his hands caught his enemy by the head. With a powerful forward heave he hurled the thug's body over his shoulder, then whirled to grapple the second man.

A pistol barked, its bullet grazing Red's arm. The next instant he had wrenched the weapon away by a swift jiu-jitsu trick, sending its owner reeling with a right hook.

"Now we'll see who's runnin' this party!" he growled. "Hands up or I'll—"

WHAP!

A blackjack wielded by the first mobster slapped Red's unprotected head. The bulky officer collapsed without a groan.

"Tha fat spy! I hope ya killed him!" rasped the man whose jaw Red had cracked. "He made my teeth ache right down to my heels!"

"Shut up and grab hold of his legs, Gimpy!" the other retorted. "If I did kill him, we got an alibi. He was threatenin' us with your gun! Anyway, we'll shove him in the garage and let the big shots worry about wakin' him up."

To carry Red's limp body across to the warehouse and through a small door at one side was a short job. A second telephone call completed the business. Immediately the pair of mobsters drove away, the bigger one still groaning about his sore jaw.

Meanwhile, in the living room of the comrades' quarters, Don Winslow was getting the real story of the beautiful Scorpion spy, Lotus. The girl had thrown away all pretense. She said she hated Scorpia and its evil plots to stir up war among the nations.

As for her own part in it, ever since she had been old enough to know right from wrong, her girlish instincts had rebelled against a life of spying and deceit. Yet her fear of Cho-San, and especially of that mysterious personage who called himself the Scorpion, had forced her to obey their orders. Even if she had dared to break with their dreaded organization, she had nowhere to go, no one to protect her from the vengeance of Scorpia.

At least, Lotus intimated, that was the situation until she had met Count Borg. André was not the criminal type she had known. He never spoke of his past life, even after she came to know him well, but he had evidently been a man of honor and high culture until joining the ranks of Scorpia.

The lonely girl had fallen desperately in love with him, though he had never acted as anything more than a kind friend to her. Whenever she whispered to him her longing to be free from Scorpia, André would show only a passing interest. Once he had half promised to take her away from Cho-San's jealous guardianship, but it never came to anything.

"And now that André is no longer one of Scorpia, he has forgotten me!" Lotus finished tearfully. "Now I will never be free, for there is no one who will help me!"

"Nonsense," exclaimed Don gruffly, trying to hide the feelings her story had roused in him. "Listen, Miss Lotus! You have a lot more real friends than you ever had before. I'm one of them, and I know of another right here in this underground stronghold of Scorpia. When you get clear, there'll be others—Uncle Sam's trusted officers and agents, men and women—who'll stand ready to protect you until we've wiped the Scorpion and Cho-San off the slate. You'll pick up your friendship with Count Borg on better terms than before. He'll be needing *you* this time, Miss Lotus—needing someone who really cares!"

"Don Winslow," answered the girl solemnly, "you've given me a hope to live for. That's something so priceless, something so far beyond any thanks, that I won't try to say more. Except that you're going to stop calling me *Miss*. Promise me that, Commander!"

"Plain Don, to you!" amended the young officer, gripping the strong little hand she offered him. "All right, Lotus; we're shipmates from now on. In the name of the United States Navy, I welcome you to the ranks of peace. But remember this, always:—*The things*

worth living for are also the things worth dying for!
You and I and Suzette—yes, she's a shipmate, too!—
may have to give our lives this very night for the cause
of world peace!"

The young girl's smile was as fearless as the light
that shone in her dark eyes.

"I am ready, Don Winslow!" she said calmly. "You
can count on me to help or to suffer, as the need may
be. Even the tortures of Cho-San's Lantern Room could
not terrify me now. Am I glad that Suzette . . ."

As if in answer to her spoken name, the little French
maid appeared from behind the carved Chinese screen.
Impulsively she seized her mistress' hands and squeezed
them.

"Suzette is glad also, Mademoiselle!" she exclaimed
earnestly. "But, *hélas!* There is no time to speak of that.
I have bad news for Commander Winslow!"

XXVI

THE ROOM OF A THOUSAND TORMENTS

Before Don could frame a question, the little French-woman caught his arm.

"*Écoutez!*" she cried in a husky undertone. "Do you know a man about twenty-six year old, with big, thick chest and red hair dyed black?"

"Yes, yes!" Don whipped back. "Go on! Tell me what you mean! They haven't caught him?"

"But they have, Monsieur!" replied Suzette. "Ah, I had the fear it might be one of your men! They have just brought him in, unconscious, and Cho-San is very much excited. I hear him say, 'Now I shall grind the truth out of that clown who calls himself Count Borg. But first, I'll burn this dog with dyed hair until he howls all he knows!' "

"It's Red!" Don groaned, his fists knotting at his sides. "You mean, Suzette, that they've got him in the torture room? Merciful heavens! I'd rather be there in his place—but, quick! Tell me what we can do to get him away?"

"There is nothing, Don!" wailed Lotus, wringing her hands in distress. "Once they have gotten your friend in the Lantern Room, there's no way of rescuing him except by a trick. The place is too well-guarded . . ."

"A trick!" exclaimed Suzette excitedly. "Let me think jus' a moment. I believe there is a way . . ."

"There's got to be!" grated Don. "Even if we lose a chance of trapping the Scorpion's whole bunch, we've got to get Red out of this. He's my shipmate, and . . ."

"Mais, oui!" cried the little maid. "We will do it with the help of *le bon Dieu!* Only first, you and Mademoiselle must be in the Lantern Room. You must pretend not to care how much they torture your poor friend. You must not let Cho-San see that you know him at all. Then, when the chance have arrive, the lights will go out. Your friend must be quickly freed, and then *Ps-st!"*

At Suzette's hissed warning, Lotus broke into rapid speech.

"I understand, my little maid!" she said loudly, with a wink at the Frenchwoman. "You think you must play the chaperon whenever I am with Count Borg. That is why you are always sneaking into the room! Now, let me tell you this . . ."

"Stop your chatter, girl!" rasped the voice of Cho-San behind them. "I have something of importance to tell your André; so be silent or leave the room! Count Borg, it appears that our task of laying hands on Don Winslow may be unexpectedly simplified!"

"Really, Cho-San!" shrugged Don indifferently. "Did you think it was going to be difficult? I imagine if you used a large enough mob to seize him . . ."

"Will you never be serious?" spat the Chinese. "To put it bluntly, in elegant words such as you can understand, we have nabbed a guy who looks like one of Winslow's pals. *Now* do you understand?"

"Oh, I say! That's luck, you know! Really!" exclaimed Don, acting his part in spite of inward anxiety. "You mean we can use this man as bait to trap Winslow? Have the fellow write a note to his Commander, or something?"

"Or something!" the Oriental mimicked him grimly. "I can think of something even simpler than a written note, my dear Count. With the information I can get from this Navy spy, by the use of a little pain . . . But come with me to the Lantern Room and see for yourself! You, too, Lotus, dismiss your maid and come with us. It is time you should see what a little persuasion—Oriental style—can accomplish. I have machines, copied from the torture rooms of Ancient China, which can extract any secret!"

Chuckling evilly, the huge Scorpion leader motioned the two young people out of the room ahead of him.

As he turned away, Don fought an overpowering desire to smash his fist into Cho-San's grinning yellow face. Only by ramming his hands deep in his pockets did he succeed in controlling them. Although on fire with anxiety for Red, he must pretend a careless, somewhat bored good humor.

"And I feared we were going to have a tiresome evening, Cho-San," he murmured. "Chinese torture machines sound awfully entertaining, I must say! Er—by the way, I don't recall how we get to the lamp room, as you call it."

"Lantern Room!" growled the Chinese. "Lotus will lead the way and I will follow. Take the shortest corridor, girl! I am anxious to see your André's face when he sets eyes on our latest captive."

The doorway concealed by the carved screen opened into another dimly lighted vestibule. Don guessed that a number of its darkly shining panels were really hidden doors, communicating with as many passageways.

The girl, however, showed no hesitation in locating the one she wanted. Her small fingers played briefly with one of the carved dragons of the molding. There was the usual muffled click. Two seconds later a black opening gaped in the solid wall.

This time the narrow corridor ran almost straight, with a sharp downward slope. The distance might have been a hundred feet before another panel slid open at Lotus' touch, and bright electric light streamed briefly into the dark passageway. Knowing, yet fearing, what he was going to see, Don Winslow stepped into the Room of a Thousand Torments.

The place was really a stone vault of immense proportions, fifty feet wide and perhaps a hundred long. Its groined ceiling was supported by thick stone pillars to which were affixed chains and ring bolts of iron.

Along the walls stood a weird array of mechanical monsters, some of them so crudely made that they might have been centuries old. Don glimpsed a medieval "rack" for pulling living human bodies apart, a rude "wheel" between whose heavy spokes human legs and arms could be broken like matchsticks, an "iron maiden" whose hinged and hollow halves were spiked with deadly knife blades.

There were rows of other horrible machines at which he barely glanced. What drew his attention like a terrible magnet was the prone figure of Red Pennington, still in his valet's garb, lying on a dark stained plank table. Blood trickling from Red's broken scalp had smeared the chalklike whiteness of his face. So deathly was his appearance that the two Chinese hatchet men standing guard above him looked like murderers gloating over their kill!

Biting hard on his tongue, Don Winslow held back his rage. Still keeping his outward pose of lazy boredom, he turned to the Scorpion leader.

"Oh, come now, Cho-San!" he protested. "What kind of a silly joke is this? The fellow's dead as dust! No fun in tormenting a corpse, you know."

With a feline hiss, Cho-San leaped past him, shouldering aside the nearest hatchet man. Placing his ear to Red's chest, he listened for the heartbeat. The silence in the great, vaulted room was breathless.

Abruptly the big Oriental straightened up, motioning the guards away.

"The man is not quite dead; we can quickly revive him," he said. "Come nearer, Count Borg! We shall show you some fun *at the expense of your own valet!*"

"What's that?" cried Don sharply, striding across to the table. "Why, you're right, Cho-San! I didn't recognize him with all that blood on his face. But see here—you can't put the screws on my valet, you know!

He's just a harmless chap I picked up to do for me . . ."

"Ummmmm-hmmmmmm! Of course, of course!" rumbled Cho-San. "Just a harmless chap you—or perhaps someone else—told to follow our car this evening! Well, my dear Count Borg, he succeeded, as you observe!"

The guards had returned with two buckets of water and a wide leather strap. At a gesture from Cho-San, they sloshed the water over Red's body from head to foot. As soon as both buckets were empty one of the hatchet men began slapping their bound and helpless victim's face with the heavy strap.

Suddenly Red groaned, rolling partly on his side. The man with the strap stepped away. At the same time, Cho-San pushed Don forward.

The trick was cleverly planned. Only luck and Don's presence of mind prevented a showdown then and there. As it happened, Red in his half-conscious state still thought he was back at the Empire rehearsing the part of "Penny."

"Yes, sir! I'll get right up, sir!" he mumbled, opening one eye. "I didn't mean to fall asleep, but . . . mmmmm —my head!"

At that moment Don flashed him a warning signal often used between them—a sharp lift of the right eyebrow. And, foggy as poor Red's brain still was, he got it.

Instead of answering, he shut his mouth and groaned. With a sigh of inward relief, Don Winslow went on with the act. Until the chance should come for a getaway, he must play for time.

"Look here, my man!" he snapped angrily. "What on earth possessed you to follow my friend's car this evening? Hang it! If this is some stupid police trick . . ."

"Not at all, my dear Count!" chortled Cho-San, seizing Red by the scalp. "It's a trick of the famous Navy Intelligence, if anything. Look closely at this stout lieutenant's hair—dyed black, *except at the roots!*"

A flat accusation could not have been more menacing than Cho-San's leer. Yet, somehow Don sensed that the Chinese was still only guessing. With a puzzled frown he returned the man's snaky gaze.

"A lieutenant?" he drawled. "Oh, of course! You mean Red Pennington. But really, Cho-San, this fellow Penny couldn't be Don Winslow's shipmate. I picked him up only today on the sidewalk, mooching for dimes. He told me he'd been a valet and I hired him. Even bought him an outfit of clothes. Come now, Cho-San, admit that your idea's a bit fantastic! Besides, how could Pennington have got here so soon from Haiti, old dear? Ha-ha! I've got you there, haven't I?"

"Unless," smiled the Chinese with sinister emphasis, "—unless you, my dear Don Winslow, brought him with you as a passenger in the plane that Michael Splendor *allowed* you to steal!"

XXVII

WHEN THE LIGHTS WENT OUT

"Oh-h-h!" Lotus' gasp of amazement was well faked. "Why, Cho-San, unless you're joking you're insane to think of such a thing! This isn't Don Winslow—it's *André!* I know because I—I love him! Even you, Cho-San, must admit a woman can recognize the man she loves."

For a moment the Scorpion leader stood snarling like a tiger that had missed its kill. His lips writhed back and strange animal sounds came through his bared yellow teeth.

"Ar-r-rgh! So!" he growled. "We shall see. We shall see if you have turned traitor to Scorpia, my little Lotus. I know one way to answer both questions. Stand aside!"

Forcing her back with a sweep of his loglike arm, Cho-San erupted into sing-song Chinese commands. While he was still speaking, the two hatchet men leaped to obey.

Red Pennington was lifted from the table, carried to a spot beneath the nearest stone arch, and held there upright, while Cho-San advanced upon him with the tread of a big jungle cat. Seizing Red's bound wrists, the Chinese jerked them toward a loop of wire which hung down from the arch's apex.

"Great guns, Lotus!" whispered Don, his lips barely moving. "We've got to do something quick. They're going to hang Red up by the thumbs—torture him before our eyes!"

The girl nodded silently. Her face was dead white, her lips a thin purple line. With Don at her side, she made for the leering Scorpion leader.

"Don't, Cho-San!" she exclaimed in a low, tragic voice. "If you are such a fiend that you must torture somebody, take me! I could stand it better than watching . . ."

"Oo-oo-oonh!"

The moan of agony was wrung from Red's lips, as Cho-San threw his weight on the pulley rope. The stocky lieutenant now hung by his thumbs from the wire loop which had cut through skin and tissue.

Only Lotus' warning nudge kept Don from throwing himself then and there upon the slant-eyed devil who was leaning on that rope. With a supreme effort he controlled himself.

Suzette, he recalled, had mentioned a plan of rescue which Lotus would attempt when the chance came. Until then he must play the game!

Lotus, he noticed, had moved over to the nearest wall. She leaned against it in a pathetic huddle, her hands covering her face. So convincing was her pose of despair that Don wondered if it were acting at all.

Red anger again clouded his brain. His hand crept to the lapel of his dinner jacket within quick reach of the automatic beneath his armpit.

"I advise you to keep your hand away from your weapon, my friend!" came Cho-San's ugly growl. "Back there in the shadows stands one of my personal bodyguards, with a Thompson submachine gun aimed at your midriff. At the first signal from me—he will make a bloody rag of your shirt front. Ah-ha! You see him now?"

Slowly Don's narrowed gaze made out the shadowy figure behind an unlighted archway. His hand lifted to cover a well-faked yawn.

"Of course I see him!" he murmured lazily. "But why all the dramatics, Cho-San? So far the fun you promised has been frightfully tiresome. I've heard men groaning in pain before in my life, you know. Really, this isn't even interesting . . ."

"It will be, my dear Borg-Winslow!" spat the Chinese. "It will be most interesting when Lieutenant Penington starts to tell us—between groans—just which your name really is! And if this simple thumb-stretcher doesn't work, I have a new electrical machine which tears the brain apart, bit by bit. Perhaps you would like me to give you a taste of that, when I am finished with your friend?"

With a ghastly chuckle, Cho-San turned back to his work. The pulley rope tightened. From Red's anguished throat burst another pitiful moan.

At that instant the huge room was plunged in darkness. There was a scuffle of feet, two hard, thudding blows—the sound of one or more falling bodies.

A girl's scream rang out, followed by Cho-San's bass

bellow. Then came silence, more stifling than the thick darkness of the vault.

In contrast to the gruesome quiet of Cho-San's dark torture room, loud argument resounded in the brightly lighted office of the local Intelligence Bureau. Michael Splendor, just arrived from the airport to take charge of operations, was laying down the law to the chief of the San Francisco operatives.

"It's all ye're fault, Hammond!" he roared, pounding the desk with an enormous hairy fist. "Ye should have seen the game was up when Cho-San butted in on the party and spirited Don Winslow away in his big black car! Ye should have had a squad of expert men ready to shadow him, instead of leavin' it to a young officer who's not trained to the work. Now, repeat if ye will, the story of that taxi driver who said he'd been hired to follow Cho-San's limousine!"

"I know he's the one who drove Pennington, because we took his license number," Hammond stated flatly. "His name's Grogan, and he seems to be on the level. He says they lost Cho-San's limousine somewhere in Chinatown. They followed another by mistake and it brought them up in front of Cho-San's curio shop. Pennington told Grogan to stop and wait while he took a look at the place. While the lieutenant was gone, two tough eggs from the second car shoved pistols through Grogan's window and told him to drive on. Grogan had no choice but to obey. He came back here to his regular stand, and we nabbed him for questioning. That's all!"

"And isn't it enough to persuade ye that both Pennington and Commander Winslow are in deadly peril?" retorted Splendor bitterly. "Why did ye have to wait till I arrived, before raidin' Cho-San's layout? Get busy, now, call up all your reserves—every fightin' man ye can deputize for the job. What's holdin' ye?"

"Nothing, sir, now that you've ordered it!" replied Hammond, his honest face flushing red. "Of course you're aware we'll need to find evidence of lawless activities in order to justify a raid. Cho-San has both wealth and influence to fight criminal charges in any court!"

"And what of that?" the lion-maned cripple roared back. "By this time Don Winslow and Pennington will have found enough evidence to hang that yellow fiend higher than Haman. Away with ye, Hammond! Collect your men, and be sure that one of them is husky enough to carry me on his back. Legs or no legs, I'll lead this raid if it's me last act!"

Without a word Hammond departed, swept from the room by the blast of Splendor's fierce energy. As the door closed behind him another opened to admit Mercedes Colby still in her flying togs.

"I heard that last, Mr. Splendor!" she cried, coming quickly to the cripple's chair. "No wonder Hammond calls you 'the old Lion'! But you were joking, weren't you, about leading this raid on Cho-San's place?"

"Faith, and why should I joke about that?" snorted

the veteran Intelligence officer. "Have I been in a jok-in' mood since we took off from Haiti this mornin'? At least I can shoot with the best of Hammond's deputies, and that's all I ask a chance to do. But what about the thing I sent ye to find out, child? Is Count Borg well guarded in that room Hammond assigned him to?"

"*Too* well guarded, if you take the Count's word for it," replied Mercedes with a smile. "Mr. Hammond assigned a couple of his best detectives, armed to the teeth, to guard the doors. Of course they didn't arm Count Borg because he's a prisoner, at least, technically. But I don't think any Scorpion gang is going to kidnap him tonight."

"I hope not, my dear," sighed Splendor, wagging his gray maned head. "But if Cho-San has pierced Don Winslow's disguise, as I fear he has done, things may happen too fast for us to prevent . . ."

"*Oh-h-h! The lights!*"

Mercedes' gasp cut through a pitch black room. Without warning every light had gone out, not only in the office building but in the street outside.

In a darkness just as absolute, Don Winslow plunged blindly forward, bearing Red's helpless weight. Lotus' scream had given him his direction. If only he didn't bump into a pillar or a prowling hatchet man, he'd make it to where she waited!

Suddenly a small, firm hand clutched his arm. Without question he obeyed its pressure, felt himself being guided past an unseen obstruction.

The next instant a cool draught struck his face. The guiding hand gave his arm one quick, farewell squeeze. Somewhere behind him sounded the click of a closing panel.

The darkness was as thick as ever, but now he sensed that he was no longer in the vaulted torture room. That cool current of air suggested a tunnel or corridor connecting with the world above ground.

Luckily he had remembered to take a small pocket torch when he went down to dinner that evening. Its white beam now showed up the rough stone walls of a passageway, like the one leading from the elevator. But that was not all.

Within arm's reach stood the French maid, Suzette, her finger to her lips in silent warning. As Don met her eyes, she beckoned urgently and turned to vanish in the black shadows.

When the flashlight found her again Suzette was several yards up the tunnel, running like a boy. Don followed somewhat more slowly, trying to keep Red's head from bumping the low, timbered roof. He was breathing heavily when he finally overtook the Frenchwoman.

"We mus' be ver' quick, Commander!" she whispered, halting at a place where the passageway branched. "Your poor friend, is he too badly hurt to walk?"

"Not so's you'd notice it, Miss!" came Red's husky

answer. "Just get these ropes off my hands and ankles, and I'll manage to toddle. Got a knife, Skipper?"

Don's penknife was already out, sawing at the brutally tight cords.

"This is easier than getting that loop of wire off your thumbs in the dark, shipmate!" he panted. "I was afraid those two cat-eyed hatchet men would come back at me before I got you clear."

"Not a chance!" grinned Red Pennington rubbing his blood smeared wrists. "You hit 'em so hard they couldn't even crawl away, Skipper. You must have judged their positions just right."

"*Allons donc, Messieurs!* We waste time!" cut in Suzette's sharp whisper. "We are not out of the danger yet. This left-hand passage—come! And run as if the devil-dog Marines were after you!"

XXVIII

PULLING DEATH'S WHISKERS

Red Pennington made a desperate spurt to catch up. His feet and hands were still numb; his head ached fiercely; his stomach was seasick for the first time in years. But that crack about the Marines was too much to swallow.

"You got it wrong, lady!" he puffed, stumbling at Suzette's heels. "You mean run like *we* were chasin' the *Marines,* don't you? No gob ever yet ran away from a leatherneck . . ."

"Pipe down and save your breath, sailor!" warned Don. "Suzette's leading this patrol, and it's not over yet by a long shot!"

As he spoke the fleet-footed French girl darted into another branch tunnel. This one doubled back after a few feet, then branched again, and continued at right angles. In the next few minutes the young officers realized they were deep in an underground maze. Here anyone but a guide with an exceptional memory would lose the way.

And now another danger made itself apparent. From time to time distant shouts and the clatter of a machine gun echoed through the rocky labyrinth. In quick whispers tossed over her shoulders Suzette urged greater speed. The noticeable dimming of Don's flashlight gave added warning.

Despite aching muscles and tortured lungs, Red forced himself to a swifter pace. As a result, he tripped and fell. Before Don could help him, he was running again, ignoring a pair of gashed knees. Sheer fighting courage kept him up, defying the weight of a body built more for comfort than for speed.

All at once Suzette slowed and stopped, throwing back a warning arm.

"Put out your torch, *Monsieur* Winslow!" she hissed. "Around the next corner is a machine gun in a 'pillbox.' It stands between us and freedom. Either we mus' silence it or be trap here where we stand!"

"I see," muttered Don. "But you must have made some plan for doing that, Suzette. What's our best play?"

In the pitch darkness the girl grasped a sleeve of each of the two men. Not until their three heads were literally together, did she reply.

"I can think of jus' one way to do," she said tensely. "Somewhere along the next passage is a photo-electric trigger, worked by infra-red light. If we try to pass it, the overhead lights flash on, the machine gunner begin to shoot, and we die with fifty bullet holes in our backs! So this, *Messieurs,* is my plan. When the lights flash on, I will empty my small pistol through the machine gunner's loophole. That will keep him busy until you pass beyond the next turn. Before he dare to look again, I follow you, and—"

"Nothing doing, Suzette!" Don cut in abruptly. "That way you'd be sacrificing your life for us and you know it. I've got another idea. We'll silence that machine gun before the lights flash up in the passageway. All I ask is for you to show me that 'pillbox' loophole *in the dark!*"

Well trained by the French Secret Service, Suzette knew the voice of authority. Without hesitation she took Don's hand.

"Come then, *Monsieur!*" she whispered. "And your friend—he mus' keep close behind us, but make no sound."

For the next thirty feet they proceeded at a snail's pace, careful not to make the slightest sound. At last, however, Suzette halted, to grope for a few seconds at an unseen wall.

Don guessed what she was doing. When the tug came on his wrist, he let his own hand be guided until it touched the edges of a square opening.

The loophole! And protruding from it, Don could feel the ugly steel snout of a submachine gun. The other end, he knew, was held by a ready killer, whose grip need only tighten on the trigger to spray forth a stream of lead and fire!

"I've heard of pulling Death's whiskers," the young officer thought with a slight shiver, "but this is the nearest I've come to doing it yet!"

His next movements were coolly calculated. Fixing the loophole's position in mind, he took a fresh grip on the unlighted pocket torch. At the same time he drew the snub-nosed .38 caliber automatic from his shoulder holster. Lastly, to steady his aim, he drew a single deep breath.

The rest happened too fast for words to describe.

The flash of Don's torch, the blast of his pistol, a muffled explosion inside the concrete wall—all followed in the same split instant. The scream of human pain that issued through the loophole seemed to be minutes later, though actually it was hardly a second.

While the cry still echoed, a blinding flood of light showed three crouched figures racing for the tunnel's end. So cramped was the passage that bullets from the "pillbox" could have cut them down like toy soldiers, but not even one shot rang out. The next instant all three had disappeared around a rocky projection of the wall.

Don Winslow's dimming flashlight now showed a rough-boarded staircase, leading upward. At Suzette's heels, the two officers mounted, three steps at a time. At the top they crossed a narrow hall, burst through a half-concealed door, and came out into the open air.

Here, in what seemed to be a dark alley, Red Pennington grabbed at Don's shoulder.

"Avast, Skipper!" he panted! "Lemme get a breath or two before we—ugh—go on!"

"*Non! Non!* Not yet, *Messieurs!*" the French-woman's voice lashed back. "Soon we will stop, but it is not safe yet. *Allons!*"

As if to confirm her words, high-pitched, Oriental voices broke out in the building behind them. Red waited for no more, but lunged ahead, sobbing for breath.

The route they followed for the next five minutes was as mixed up as the maze of underground tunnels they had left. Back and forth through dark alleyways and darker buildings they dodged. Suzette had evidently studied the route by daylight, and kept a map of it in her mind for just such an emergency.

At the last door, which seemed to be that of a basement apartment, she used a key.

"This place is safe if we do not show the light, *Messieurs*," she panted. "Many weeks ago I have rent and furnish it under another name. Beyond is a door opening to another street where you can get a taxi. And now, while Suzette gets her breath, tell me what you did to that machine gun, Commander. I die of curiousness!"

"I took a chance and tried to plug his gun muzzle with my own bullet," Don answered. "Just by luck I did it first try. Of course, when the machine gunner pulled the trigger, his weapon blew up! That's all there was to it!"

"Except a chilled steel nerve and cracking good marksmanship!" grunted Red Pennington. "If you'd missed that first shot the guy inside would have blown your head off."

"*Mais, oui!*" chimed in Suzette. "We owe our lives to the so brave Commander! But now I mus' speak of other things. Tell me, Monsieur Winslow, how many men you can bring for a raid tonight on the under-

world of Scorpia? We mus' strike now, while so many
agents are here for Cho-San's big conference!"

"You're right, Suzette!" exclaimed Don. "Tonight's
the time, and I've asked our local office to hold fifty
fighting men within call in case I needed them. Michael
Splendor has just arrived and is probably running them
up now. I could lead them back here within an hour,
probably . . ."

"But that is perfect, Commander!" cried the little
Frenchwoman. "Go now, and bring your men to the
shop of Cho-San. I will have the door unlock, so you
need make no noise. From the shop I will conduct you
to the secret gallery w'ich overlook the Scorpion's great
Assembly Room. The agents will soon be gather there
to hear Cho-San's instructions for a new world war
plot. Your men will then take them by surprise and
make the—w'at you call—*clean-up* in one big swoop!"

"We'll do that or die trying, Suzette!" Don exclaimed
heartily. "Now lead the way to the other door, and
we'll be off. If you get a chance to speak to Lotus, tell
her we'll be back to take her away from Cho-San's torture rooms and slimy passages."

Suzette did not reply. Taking Don's hand she led the
two young officers swiftly through the apartment and
an adjoining basement. As they came out onto a darkened areaway, Don Winslow thought he heard the little
maid sob.

"Voila!" she said in a choked voice. "You can see the
street beyond that alley to the right. And hurry, *Messieurs,* if you hope to see the little Lotus alive. I have

fear that Cho-San has punish her already for her part in helping you escape!"

Don's groan came through gritted teeth.

"Heaven grant you're wrong about that!" he said hoarsely. "If that child has given her life for us, we'll never rest till we wipe the last memory of Scorpia from the earth! Come, Red! Every second counts against us now!"

XXIX

THE WRATH OF CHO-SAN

Feet stamped and flashlights blazed through the office building of the local Intelligence Bureau. Above the sounds of disciplined search, Michael Splendor's great voice could be heard roaring questions and orders.

There had been two or three minutes time, however, between the moment the lights went out and the organization of a flashlight brigade. In that brief space the emissaries of Scorpia had pulled off their carefully planned raid and departed. As souvenirs of their visit they had left two drugged and unconscious detectives outside an upper floor room.

Count Borg had vanished, snatched from under the noses of Hammond's best men; and no one had seen him go. The fact was a stunning blow to the Bureau chief; but to Splendor, it was just one more challenge to fight.

"Find out how many men ye've got here now, Hammond!" he bellowed down the corridor. "Bring them back to the main office so I can look them over. If I spot no spies among them, we'll start at once."

The office lights were still out, but darkness was no obstacle to the gray-haired cripple. Holding an electric torch in his teeth, he propelled his wheel chair through the door and around the long oak table which ran almost the length of the room. Satisfied that no prowlers lurked in the shadows, he took his place beside the single entrance and waited.

Moments later, Hammond finished rounding up his force of deputies. As he led them down the corridor toward the main office Splendor's bull voice hailed him.

"Stand opposite me, Hammond," the veteran ordered, "and let your men pass between us one by one. That way we'll be sure there's no traitor among them!"

As he spoke there was a sudden stir among the group of men outside. It ended briefly with a cry of discovery.

"I've got him, sir!" cried one of the deputies. "This fellow didn't want to stand inspection, I guess. I caught him trying to slip away!"

Spotlighted by a score of torch beams, the culprit was pushed forward to the door. In his light topcoat he looked like a slim boy, hanging his head as if in shame.

A flick of Hammond's hand knocked off the low pulled fedora and brought a gasp from every onlooker. The youthful face, under a mass of tightly wound hair, was Mercedes Colby's.

"I don't care—I'm going with you anyway!" the girl exploded, turning upon Michael Splendor. "I'm no fluffy, helpless child to be sent to bed when there's a real job of work to do! If a man with no legs can risk his life to help Don Winslow, so can a girl. And you're not going to stop me!"

Throwing off the borrowed topcoat, Mercedes stood there slim and defiant in her boyish flying togs. Her clear eyes glowed like battle lanterns in the light of Splendor's torch beam. Before the veteran could frame a reply, a voice outside in the corridor drew everyone's attention.

"Good for you, Mercedes!" cried Don Winslow, striding up the corridor with Red at his heels. "You're not the only woman who's risking her life tonight in the cause of humanity. When he knows the truth, even Mr. Splendor won't try to keep you back!"

Don's arrival acted like a powerful stimulant to the spirits of everyone there. What had seemed a dangerous duty to most of Hammond's hard-boiled deputies, now took on the color of high adventure. There was something in the young Commander's presence which always fired men to eager loyalty, and they expressed it now in a muffled cheer.

Briefly Don outlined the situation up to the moment he and Red had left Suzette. In return Hammond told him of Count Borg's disappearance, and the preparations made up to then.

Each deputy, the Bureau chief explained, was armed with two pistols. Half of them carried Thompson submachine guns and the rest a supply of tear gas bombs. There were extra weapons and gas masks in the office, he said, from which Don and Red could choose.

"I can't see that there's any need to wait, then," said Don. "As soon as Mr. Splendor has finished his inspection, we can start!"

For weapons, both the Navy officers selected regulation Enfield rifles, which could be used as terrible clubs in hand-to-hand fighting. Mercedes, still insistent on going along, was fitted out with a bulletproof vest under her light topcoat. Her weapons consisted of a pair of automatics, one loaded with tear gas cartridges. The three of them were the last to pass Michael Splendor's swift inspection.

At his own signal, the veteran was lifted pickaback to the shoulders of a powerful deputy, and carried at the head of his fifty men to the cars waiting outside. With a few low spoken words, the deputies jammed into the vehicles. Doors slammed, starters whirred, and the raiding party was on its way, speeding through the foggy streets.

Twenty minutes later, the leading car braked to a stop in front of Cho-San's darkened shop. As the others lined up behind it, the crippled but dauntless leader headed the silent rush of fighting men across the street.

At the shop door Don and Red caught up with him. The knob turned easily at the young Commander's touch. An instant later ten flashlight beams picked out the small figure of Suzette, waiting in the center of the room.

"Thank Heaven you are arrive, *Messieurs!*" the girl exclaimed. "The little Lotus still lives, and they have just brought in Count Borg. Follow me quickly if you would save them!"

Deep under the fortresslike mansion of Cho-San, a huge room had been hollowed out of the native earth and rock. Across one end of it stretched a platform, equipped with lights to produce every sort of stage effect. The room's main floor space was filled with regular theater seats enough to accommodate two hundred persons.

At present more than half of the seats were occupied. Men and women of all nationalities sat conversing in twenty different tongues and dialects. As if to add drama to the scene, each appeared in his native costume, however outlandish it happened to be. There were dark men from India, Morocco, and the South Sea Islands; black men from Africa, and yellow men from the Far East. Mingled with these were fair-skinned women from North and South America and from the glittering capitals of Europe—a strangely varied and colorful assembly!

Yet for all their differences of age, sex and race, these people had one trait in common. It was an expression of reckless cruelty, like a brand burned deep into their very souls.

There was nothing strange about that, of course, for these were the key men and women of Scorpia, the chief spies and agents of a world-wide crime club. Success for them meant always disaster for civilized nations—revolutions, wars, and bloody conquests, from which the Scorpion's brood could pick their illegal wealth.

The sound of hard-voiced laughter and conversation died suddenly. Weird music throbbed out from some hidden source. Slowly the great curtain of purple velvet rolled back upon a scene of medieval horror.

Three spotlights threw a merciless radiance upon the darkened stage. In the center stood Cho-San, robed in the rich silks of Ancient China, his hands clasped under loose sleeves. Motionless as a statue, his huge figure dominated the scene.

At Cho-San's right a second spotlight circled a great wooden wheel, to whose spokes had been lashed the body of a girl. Still clad in her white satin evening gown, Lotus' young beauty was in tragic contrast with her stiff, tortured pose.

The third part of the gruesome tableau was a heavy wooden stretcher, or rack, to which a man was bound by hands and feet. So taut were the ropes that another turn of the machine's windlass would have jerked his joints apart.

All this the audience took in before the first gasp of astonishment escaped their lips. Like a wind through dry branches a harsh whisper swept across the room:—

"The Lotus! Count Borg! *What does it mean, Cho-San?*"

The whisper died into silence. Openmouthed the assembled agents of Scorpia sat staring at the terrible, unspoken wrath of Cho-San. As they watched, the towering figure of the Chinese seemed to swell and palpitate with voiceless fury.

When it came, his first word rolled out like an organ's shuddering bass.

"Treason!" he thundered. "Treason to the power of Scorpia! These two, about to die in torment, dared to defy the Master; and I, Cho-San, accuse them before you all!"

XXX

TRAPPED

The hundred-odd men and women of Scorpia shivered in the darkness beyond the stage. All had heard tales of Cho-San's torture room. Some even had visited the vaulted chamber and seen old bloodstains on those devilish machines.

They remembered their fellow agents who had disappeared to be "tried" later in this same underground auditorium. In such cases the accused were brought on the stage to give their "confessions"; but their broken bodies and fear stricken tones told plainer than words of secret torments. Not even the few who were released after trial ever told exactly what had happened to them.

And now these members of Scorpia's Inner Council were to see with their own eyes the fate of two who had defied the Scorpion's power. Their cruel natures were as thrilled by the prospect as they were awed by thought that their own turn might come some day.

Such was the mind of the audience which heard Cho-San's grim accusation. With savage eagerness they drank in the Scorpion leader's every word, while their eyes gloated over those helpless victims on the wheel and rack.

With the tread of a great jungle beast, Cho-San approached the half-conscious Lotus.

Facing the assembly, the Chinese raised his voice.

"This girl, this fickle traitoress," he cried, "has gone over to the enemy, body and soul. In a few minutes you will hear her confess her guilt under mortal pain. But first—"

Cho-San paused dramatically.

"First," he repeated, "she will listen to the screams of this other enemy of Scorpia—the man who was once a member of this very Inner Council—Count André Borg! We shall see what confession another turn of the ropes will wring from him . . . Dr. Skell!"

Into the spotlight moved a tall man garbed in a white laboratory coat. His bald, skull-like head turned to face Cho-San.

"One turn?" he asked, laying a bony hand upon the rack's windlass.

The Chinese nodded. Slowly the rack's wooden crank moved downward, tightening the ropes. Count Borg's body stiffened under the frightful tension. Through his clenched jaws issued a grinding sob of pain.

"Another turn and his bones snap out of their sockets," came the dry croak of Dr. Skell. "Shall I go on?"

"No! No!" came Lotus' frantic cry. "Torture me, Cho-San, but not André! Anything—*anything but that!*"

"Tear him apart!" snarled the Scorpion leader. "Put your weight on that windlass, or—"

CR-RACK!

The whipping report of a rifle slapped against the walls. With a queer, animal whine, the bony Skell shrank back, his bullet grazed hand dripping red.

For a moment paralysis seemed to grip the assembled Council of Scorpia. Then through tense silence the voice of Don Winslow cut like a knife.

"Hold it, Cho-San! We've got every exit covered. You'd better give up!"

Quick as a cat, the big Chinese leaped. Outside the spotlight, his figure was a swift vanishing blur. The slam of an automatic pistol came seconds too late, as Michael Splendor charged onto the stage at the head of twenty fighting men.

Leaping down across the footlights, Don Winslow, Red Pennington and a dozen of Hammond's men lined up with ready guns. Yet in the face of that threat more than half the Scorpion assembly had drawn concealed pistols.

A single shot would touch off a battle to the death. None knew it better than Michael Splendor as he perched on the shoulders of a powerful deputy, full in the spotlight's glare. He knew also that men and women, however desperate, can sometimes be bluffed.

"Every exit to this room is blocked by armed men!" he announced in a ringing voice. "Throw down your weapons and ye'll take no harm. Fight and ye'll get licked anyway. Which will ye choose?"

A low muttering began among the trapped council-men of Scorpia. Above the babel of whispers a single voice rose clear.

"Cho-San escaped!" rang the defiant shout. "The se-cret corridors are NOT blocked. We will scatter—and catch these fools in their own trap!"

A roar of approval went up from the crowd. In three scrambling groups the assembly broke for the sides and rear of the auditorium, avoiding the platform. A few of the nearest kept their eyes and pistols trained on the line of riflemen, but they clearly wished to postpone the shooting.

To the mob's angry surprise, this means of escape had been forestalled. When the paneled exit doors slid back, a squad of deputies barred each opening with clubbed guns. At the same time Splendor's bellow rose above the tumult.

"On with your gas masks, boys!" he ordered. "We'll have these wastrels chokin' for breath in two minutes."

Suiting action to words, the veteran pulled the ring of a tear gas grenade and flung it. Twice more he re-peated the motion before bullets from the ranks of Scorpia drilled him and his human mount. With a groan the big deputy sank to his knees, spilling his wounded chief to the floor.

From the embattled exits more gas grenades were being hurled, but there the press of fighting bodies was too close for pistol work. The same sort of struggle was taking place where Don Winslow and his squad of fighters held back a rush for the stage exits.

The only shooting appeared to be aimed at Splendor and the fallen deputy, sprawled in the white glare of the spotlight.

It was Mercedes Colby who acted in the nick of time to save them. Already she had cut loose the racked body of Count Borg and freed his sobbing companion. Now, braving the bullets that clipped across the stage, she started to drag Michael Splendor out of the light.

At that moment two Malay councilmen broke through Don's thin line of fighting deputies. Maddened by the smart of tear gas they leaped onto the platform, armed with long, glittering knives. Their yells of tiger-ish fury announced that they had gone *amok*.

Bullets could not have stopped them in time, yet Mercedes sprang to face them. Her left hand pistol barked. White smoke from the tear gas cartridges belched in the face of her attackers.

Their yells ended in choking grunts. Clawing at their blinded eyes, the Malays staggered back to plunge over the platform's edge.

XXXI

THE SECRET CHAMBER

From then on it was a losing battle for the Scorpion forces. The tear gas, now filling the entire room, effectively blinded everyone but the masked raiders. One after another the furious councilmen gave up the struggle to nurse their swollen eyes.

Don Winslow sensed the turn of the tide. Turning back, he leaped onto the stage which was still clear of the fumes, and raised his mask.

"Give up, you dupes of Scorpia!" he shouted. "All those who have had enough, come this way!"

There was an instant rush toward the platform. With streaming, smarting eyes, the men and women of Cho-San's erstwhile audience fought their way toward the sound of Don's voice, glad to surrender. The only ones who stayed back were the twenty or more who had run into a hard-swung gun butt, and lay snoring where they had dropped.

Of Hammond's deputies, however, ten men were wounded by knives or bullets, and three had given their lives. Don Winslow and Red each bled from knife slashes received in the melee. The old lion, Michael Splendor, had taken a bullet through the throat, but he still lived by a miracle. Mercedes, with Lotus' help, had just finished bandaging the veteran's wound when Don located them back stage. Count Borg lay near by, conscious but unable to rise.

The problem now was to evacuate safely both walking persons and wounded. Don himself had just turned back to take charge when the little French maid, Suzette, appeared suddenly out of the shadows.

"Come with me, *Monsieur,*—you and two others!" she cried, seizing the young Commander's arm. "I have locate Cho-San and Scorpion himself in their secret chamber. They are prepare now the getaway with their treasure and secret papers. In a few moments they will be gone!"

Red Pennington and Mercedes were near enough to overhear. Their response was instantaneous.

"We're with you, Don!" they said, almost together.

From the other side of the platform a big man was approaching, his tommy-gun held across an arm. As the newcomer raised his gas mask, Don hailed him.

"Hammond! Take charge of clearing out prisoners and wounded!" he ordered. "Get Mr. Splendor out first. We'll see you topside."

Before the Bureau Chief could answer Don turned, heading into the stage wing at Suzette's heels. Mercedes and Red followed, stowing away their gas masks as they ran. If more fighting were ahead of them, they would need free hands and clear eyesight.

Suzette led them through a rapid succession of passageways and sliding panels, without stopping for explanations. Not until all four of them had crowded into a tiny elevator and shut the door, did she answer any of the questions in the others' minds.

"We are now descending to the basement of Cho-San's big house," she whispered. "This is the way he escaped a few minutes ago. I guess where he have gone, and follow him by a roundabout way. I listen and hear him talk with the Scorpion in the secret chamber. Now if we are quick . . ."

The elevator stopped with scarcely a bump. As the door slid open, Don stepped out, his rifle at the ready. The others piled out after him, into a large, magnificently furnished room.

"This is the Scorpion's study," hissed Suzette. "The hidden chamber is beyond that tall mirror. Come, and keep your weapons ready."

Once across the big room, the Frenchwoman motioned the others to take up positions on each side of the long *cheval* glass. The moment they had done so, she pressed a hidden spring.

Without a sound the mirror tilted outward from the top to show a small, lighted room beyond. A glimpse of two men in overcoats standing beside an open safe was enough for Don. His rifle swung up to cover them, just as the door mechanism stopped halfway open with a click.

At the sound both men spun around, their hands too full to reach for a weapon. Cho-San's right arm held a bundle of black bound ledgers, his left hand a heavy satchel. His leer of fury was devilish. The other man's face was masked by a purple cloth. Beneath the sleeves of the black overcoat, his gloved hands gripped a pair of suitcases.

For ten seconds the tableau held, in an atmosphere charged with menace. Strangely enough, it was Suzette's half sobbing cry that broke the tension.

"Hélas, Monsieur!" wailed the little Frenchwoman. "I cannot make the door open more!"

"Never mind, Suzette," came Don's calm reply. "I've got the Scorpion covered. Cho-San, if you can lower that door from the inside, better do it and give up peaceably. You can't dodge the rifle Pennington has aimed at you."

"Very well, Winslow," the big Chinese growled, letting fall his armful of ledgers. "I'll have to use a key to release the mechanism."

Coolly Cho-San slipped a hand into his overcoat pocket. As he withdrew it, Don caught the light of a small, shiny object. Without warning it flicked from the yellow fingers, straight toward the half-open door.

Smoke puffed in a sudden cloud, obscuring the whole opening. From behind it came a harsh mocking laugh.

Before the sound died out, Don Winslow slammed his rifle barrel into the crack of the closing mirror, jamming its machinery. At the same time there came the clang of a steel door somewhere inside the secret room.

"They're gone!" yelped Red Pennington. "Quick, Suzette! Which way can we follow 'em?"

"Back! Get back, *Monsieur!*" cried the little French maid, tugging at his sleeve. "That smoke is deadly poison. Quick, everyone—put on the gas masks and come away!"

"She's right, Red!" clipped Don Winslow, whipping out his own mask. "Clear out of here before something worse happens! I'll be with you as soon as I get my gun loose."

The smoke had spread out some distance from the jammed doorway, making objects near it indistinct. As his friends moved back, Don Winslow plunged straight into it. For a few moments his figure vanished completely.

Just as Red was about to go back for him he reappeared, carrying not only his rifle but a bundle of black leather-covered books. Without lifting his mask, he motioned the others on, away from the spreading smoke.

For Suzette, their retreat was barely in time. Unprotected by a gas mask, the courageous French girl had refused to leave the room before Don appeared. Now, reeling from a slight dose of the poison, she led them through a panel in the farther wall.

In the clean air of an adjoining room she motioned her companions to remove their masks.

"It is over now, my friends," she said faintly, as Red steadied her in the grip of a muscular arm. "We have lost the Scorpion and his so evil lieutenant, but we have fail in nothing else, I think. Thanks to Commander Winslow, we have the evidence which will convict many of our enemies of their hidden crimes!"

Following her eloquent look, Mercedes let out a muffled cry.

"So that's what you went back for, Don?" she gasped. "You—you went into that gas filled room just for those black ledgers? Oh, why did you do it?"

"Cho-San seemed to value them, and I knew he couldn't have stopped to pick them up," the young commander answered. "If they do contain the evidence Suzette claims, they're worth a bigger risk than I took. And, speaking of risks, we're none of us out of here yet. For all we know the next room to this may be filled with hachet men waiting to jump us."

"*Mais non,*" cried Suzette, catching Mercedes' startled look. "I think Cho-San sent all the hachet men and bodyguards ahead to help them with their getaway. When they leave that secret chamber, they go by some other passage to the outside. No doubt the cars were waiting to take them and their men. Jus' now this house is safe as any church."

Mercedes Colby slipped an arm around the little maid's waist.

"Perhaps you're right, Suzette," she smiled, "but even that doesn't make me anxious to stay here. Lean your weight on me and let's get going. Fresh air is what we need more than anything, except news from our friends."

The news that reached them at the local Intelligence Office was better than Don Winslow or any of his three companions had dared to expect. The bullet which had passed through Michael Splendor's throat had missed the large blood vessels, though coming dangerously near to the spinal cord. The doctors' first report gave him more than a fighting chance to live.

Count Borg's wrenched limbs would be useless for the next month, but his agony on the rack had somehow torn the veil obscuring his memory. His first words on regaining consciousness had been an anxious question about Lotus. The girl herself was at the same hospital, suffering from shock, but happier than she had been in her life before.

Red Pennington refused point-blank to be doctored at the hospital. He insisted that Don with a first aid kit could fix up his torn thumbs and bruised head as well as any sawbones. He'd go to the hospital next day, he declared, but as a visitor, not a patient.

Actually it was two days before the doctors permitted the two young officers and Mercedes Colby to visit the crippled veteran. By that time the danger of wound fever was past, and the "Old Lion" of the Navy Intelligence Service was loudly demanding a sight of his friends.

"Ahoy, Commander!" he greeted, as Don stepped into the white hospital room. "They showed me your note about the evidence in those black ledger books. Is it true that it clinches the guilt of all them we took in the raid?"

"It does more than that, sir!" smiled Don, taking the older man's hand. "But I'm not going to tell you another thing till you calm down and quit trying to sit up. A man with a bullet hole in his vertebrae . . ."

"Whisht, now!" complained the dauntless cripple. "Is

that a respectful way to talk to your elders? Mercedes, child! Tell me what's on Commander Winslow's mind. Suspense is not good for a sick man, ye know that!"

"Lie down and I'll tell you!" laughed the girl, taking the chair Red had moved over to the bedside. "It's just that those ledgers contain a record of every order carried out by Scorpion agents in the past two years. The evidence incriminates hundreds more besides those we captured two nights ago."

"Yeah!" put in Red Pennington with a fighting grin. "With this evidence as a weapon, the United States Navy is going to make a thorough clean-up on the Scorpion! Am I right, Skipper?"

"I hope so, Red!" replied Don Winslow soberly. "At least we'll make the Americas and their two oceans an unlucky harbor for the enemies of peace. With the aid of all our loyal shipmates, not forgetting Suzette and Count Borg and Lotus, too, we'll work, we'll live, and if need be we'll die to make this old world a better place!"

"Amen!" responded Michael Splendor from his sickbed. "Already ye have the Scorpion and his warmongers on the run, but perilous waters lie before ye, Commander. The enemy is desperate. He'll use every fiendish trick to wreck ye, and there'll be a bitter fight when ye overhaul him—perhaps in some far corner of the earth. Me one regret is that I must lie here safe and helpless for the next two months while me young shipmates are riskin' their necks on land or sea or in the air!"

Impulsively Don gripped Splendor's big hand with both his own.

"You old fire-eater!" he exclaimed. "You'll be back with us *inside* of two months, if my guess is right! Not even a bullet nicked spine is going to keep you out of our country's fight to wipe war—and the threat of war —from the face of the earth."

"May your words come true!" replied the crippled veteran earnestly. "And may victory crown your every venture, Don Winslow of the Navy!"

THE END

Watch for the next Don Winslow story!